The Squabble

The Squabble

Nikolai Gogol

Translated by Hugh Aplin

ET REMOTISSIMA PROPE

100 PAGES

100 PAGES
Published by Hesperus Press Limited
4 Rickett Street, London sw6 1ru
www.hesperuspress.com

First published by Hesperus Press Limited, 2002

Introduction and English language translation © Hugh Aplin, 2002
Foreword © Patrick McCabe, 2002

Designed and typeset by Fraser Muggeridge
Printed in the United Arab Emirates by Oriental Press

isbn: 1-84391-013-6

CONTENTS

FOREWORD

Battle Beyond the Stars

In 1980, science fiction was hot. Films such as *The Empire Strikes Back* and *Alien* had rocked the box office. *Battlestar Galactica* sold a million toys. It was only a matter of time before Hollywood studios, desperate for product, placed a call to legendary B-movie maverick Roger Corman, who, after a thirty-year career, had succeeded in establishing himself as king of the drive-in with quickie movies like *Little Shop of Horrors* and *Bucket of Blood*. Within days, the fastest producer on the West Coast was to find himself facing his biggest undertaking yet – donning the magic glasses of a great Russian writer and, with their assistance, providing the masses with a comic-nightmare depiction of the world and the human condition such as had never before been seen, in the most lurid of widescreen Eastmancolor, complete with theatrical trailer – 'See! Thwarted love, blind hatred! See! Catastrophic misunderstanding! See! Parables of mutual destruction!' – destined for distribution throughout the grind houses of America, complete with wagonloads of promotional material specially commissioned in the brashest of comic-book styles. It would be called *Battle Beyond the Stars*, and in a feat of impish reversed anticipation worthy of its subject would concern itself not in the slightest with space mercenaries, rogue asteroids and the like, but with the comings and goings of two gentlemen of the little Ukrainian town of Mirgorod, the script to be provided by a fresh new young talent, the theatrically inclined son of a small landowner from the 'bright and muddy' market town of Sorochintsy, Province of Poltava, Little Russia, named Nikolai, born, perhaps not insignificantly, on the 1st of April, whose most distinguishing feature happened to be a very dangerous-looking nose, and whose aliens were destined to be of a much more familiar hue, bumptiously disporting themselves in frock-coats and twills – not to mention gold-brocaded jackets! – upon that place we call 'this island earth'.

The collaboration proved to be the achievement of Corman's career, surpassing even *Attack of the Crab Monsters*, and was instrumental in consolidating the career of the young Nikolai Gogol, who, up until then, had been seen primarily as a realist, and now found himself in great demand, with shoals of invitations arriving daily, offering work on any number of projects, chief among them Rod Serling's *Twilight Zone*, *The Outer Limits*, and, most perspicaciously of all, as the author himself was later to observe, *Laurel and Hardy's All-new Intergalactic Adventure*.

All of which was fine, except that whatever was to become of these audacious adventures in the scriptwriting trade, I am afraid we are never to know, for they are to be found only in a place forever inaccessible to the likes of you and me – the nebulous, intangible vortexes of our neighbourhood parallel universe, which, up until recently, even the most learned scientists were wont to pour scorn on, mirthfully deriding all who might dare to claim otherwise – such as readers of *Astounding Tales*, for example, or *The Flash*. What a surprise, then, to discover that not only do they exist, but they do so in their myriad number! And not just that – but have transpired to be very similar in form to those imagined in print by a certain long-nosed author who thought nothing of that olfactory organ turning up inside bread rolls before driving off in carriages to set up house on the moon. 'Yes,' we are now told – see BBC TV's *Horizon* programme February 2002 – by the 'learned personages', as Gogol, no doubt, would term them: 'There indeed are very close-by possible universes where, for example, Elvis Presley might still be alive, or in another, the British Empire might be going strong.'

And in which, it might be added, earnest Gogolian scholars such as yourself will eagerly grip these pages as they sombrely peruse them in the hope of gaining further enlightenment in the field of Russian literature – but it won't, in fact, be *you*, gentle reader. For the simple fact that *you* won't be there!

It is all, apparently, to do with something called the 'String Theory' and the capacity of atomic particles to exist simultaneously in different locations, suggesting that there indeed may be an infinite number of universes, each with a different law of physics – the mysterious worlds, it surely must be, concealed from us, just there beyond our senses, of which the mystics have so long spoken and in whose topsy-turvy, 'weird physics' towns, pioneers such as Dudley D. Watkins – creator of Lord Snooty and Desperate Dan in *The Beano*, with his transformed Dundee aka Cactusville and Bunkerton, complete with street lamps, postboxes and steamrollers, surely a fully paid-up Gogolian – would appear contentedly to reside. Other inhabitants must surely include *Shock Corridor's* Sam Fuller (his 16mm travelogue-style waterfall in this film seems to come crashing out of nowhere in the same delicious manner as Gogol's inspired, paint-splashing eruptions of poetry and expanded metaphor), David *Blue Velvet/Mulholland Drive* Lynch, and Gualtiero Jacopetti, creator of *Mondo Cane*: artists who have consistently identified themselves as being more than happy to shriek with comparable delight and savage irony in this eerily familiar land where sudden unexpected swerves in the direction of parody and the irrational are commonplace, with verbal and visual nightmare fireworks exploding all around them, each one, however elliptically or idiosyncratically – but always, most of all, mischievously (well, not Dudley D., perhaps, but Snitch and Snatch seem in some way father to the man) – exploring what Joyce Carol Oates has identified as, 'The subjectivity that is the essence of the human [which] is also the mystery that divides us irrevocably from one another.'

What then, having accepted the wide-ranging influence of an artist, said by Nabokov to be possessed of the true strangeness of genius, are we now to make of the Socialist Realists of the thirties and forties for whom Nikolai Gogol was 'a progressive and realistic writer who forged his works as weapons to be used against the prevailing social order'? Was it any wonder the poor man went mad? Are we to be surprised that he ended up screaming, with spirits being poured over his head, hot loaves applied to his person, and leeches attached to his nose, having had to put up with this kind of cod for the greater part of his creative life? All we can do is give thanks that there exists, on this particle called Earth and in this particular free-floating universe, a mind like that of his neighbour (Gogol wasn't Russian – even the language was an acquired tongue, a fact which is frequently overlooked, and not at all without significance when examining his unique style – and knew far less about Russia than the 'Social Realist' school might care to admit), one Vladimir Nabokov, whose mind happily was bountifully endowed with common sense as much as genius, and who never hesitated to take a swipe at this kind of enfeebled nonsense. 'Russian progressive critics,' he writes in his near-masterpiece – *Nikolai Gogol* (New Directions, 1961), certainly one of the finest books by a writer on the craft of writing – 'sensed in him [Akaky Akakyevich] the image of the underdog and the whole story ['The Greatcoat'] impressed them as a social protest. But it is something much more than that. The gaps and black holes in the texture of Gogol's style imply flaws in the texture of life itself. Something is very wrong and all men are mild lunatics engaged in pursuits that seem to them very important while an absurdly logical force keeps them at their futile jobs – this is the real "message" of the story.' He goes on astutely to observe that the difference between the comic side of things and the cosmic depends solely upon one sibilant, the prose of Gogol evoking sensations which are at once both ludicrous and stellar.

What seems most extraordinary, though, bearing this refreshing assessment in mind, is that the tale of the two Ivans which succeeds these few humble meditations ought to have been so cursorily summarised by such an eminent and empathetic critic as 'the best of his purely humorous tales', for if 'The Squabble' or 'The Tale of How Ivan Ivanovich Fell Out with Ivan Nikiforovich' is purely humorous, then I am afraid that it is incumbent upon me shamefully to disclose that as I delicately withdraw my writing instrument from its obligingly accommodating inkpot, I do so with the commendably sculpted talons of a webbed foot – for I am a goose, dear reader, or, if you prefer, a gander. There can be few narratives in any language – certainly none that I have come across – which so heartbreakingly anatomise the circumstances which give rise to the 'spiritual disharmony' and the 'whole of life grotesquely out of balance' of which Carson McCullers wrote, and Tolstoy's 'meaningless absurdity of life which is the only incontestable knowledge known to man'.

In the tale before us then, who is this narrator who seems privy to even the most intimate of thoughts and actions? Is he, perhaps Blake's Nobodaddy, or The Evil One, Satan's home- and hell-bound agent, as Chichikov in *Dead Souls* would appear to be? Remember, it was a conceit of the author's to attire his horned monsters and hoofed devils in the garb of petty miscreants, imbuing them with the attitudes of vaguely knavish small-town officials, and our weary and regretful one – or is that, thinly veiled, the sound of gleeful, mocking laughter? – may well be such a chucklesome, shadow-world wanderer.

Or, as seems more likely, is he, in fact, Gogol himself – that troubled soul who, as a child, fled shrieking from caterpillars, and in later life ran hunted from demons of a more insidious and destructive kind, those residing within himself – and who said of his own work that he was so plagued by depression that his gift for mimicry and comic exaggeration provided him with relief from these 'unaccountable fits'.

Certainly it is undeniable, as has been suggested – predictably enough, given their shared tendency towards caricature and bathos – that there is something of Dickens in this man's work, with his endless parade of shyster lawyers, amiable swindlers and doltish bureaucrats. But when the Little Russian's troika decides to leave the path and determinedly sets forth on its own journey – forsaking, in other words, the safe road of the rational, with no safety net in sight, and neither roars of applause nor condemnation ringing in his ears – whatever comparison there might be surely comes to an end, and there is simply no one in the galaxy of literature who can even begin to approach him, as his sturdy steeds lift their wings, and he soars, triumphal chariot whirling up the dust.

And in this fabulous tale – for that is surely what it is, a fantastic, self-parodic, mock-heroic folk-tale on drugs in outer space – his carriage is most certainly galloping (the reinsman's keen sense of civic responsibility – that tragic self-delusion which practically destroyed his art and, unquestionably, hastened his demise – but the distant memory of some ill-advised, if well-meaning, old fool) from this island earth to the furthest star, there encountering two cosmic ciphers, colossal twin Mutt and Jeffs in their antics and japes separated but conjoined – (in some futile search, it might be advanced, for The Noses who live on the moon) – circling the heavens, as some eternal Catherine wheel of flesh, with the sparks of their curses perpetually dying, but condemned to be reborn, out there amongst the planets – secure in but one single truth, that of their irrevocable exile – self-inflicted, like our own – from a place they'd known so well, now only faintly remembered as Paradise.

– Patrick McCabe, 2002

The three stories in this book all date from the middle of the 1830s. 'Olde-Worlde Landowners' and 'The Squabble' were both included in the two volumes of Gogol's *Mirgorod* in 1835 (although 'The Squabble' had already appeared in a miscellany a year earlier), while 'The Carriage' was originally published in 1836 in the first issue of Alexander Pushkin's journal, *The Contemporary*. Work on the three stories took place between the end of 1832 and the beginning of 1836, and thus, broadly speaking, simultaneously with work on the majority of the stories that are often grouped together as 'the Petersburg Tales' – 'Nevsky Avenue', 'The Portrait', 'Notes of a Madman', and 'The Nose' (although the best-known story in the cycle, 'The Greatcoat', was written slightly later). And just as these latter works are generally viewed as representing something of a unity, most obviously in terms of their setting, so the three stories here could justifiably be labelled 'the Little Russian tales', sharing, as they do, various characteristics, including their use of a Little Russian or Ukrainian backcloth.

Nikolai Gogol was, of course, Ukrainian by birth, and his literary debut in prose reflected that fact. The two volumes of *Evenings on a Farmstead Near Dikanka* published in 1831 and 1832 were packed full of motifs from Ukrainian daily life and folklore, and were at least in part inspired by the enthusiasm of Russian readers of the day for literature enlivened with an often somewhat artificial ethnographic local colour. For all the originality of Gogol's creative imagination, he was, at the beginning of his career, prone to seek success by following current literary fashion, sometimes with disastrous results: the first work he published as a separate edition was a narrative poem, the most important genre in Russian literature in the

1820s, but one for which the aspirant author showed very little talent; the historical tale in the *Mirgorod* collection, 'Taras Bulba', responded to the 1830s' vogue for novels in the manner of Sir Walter Scott without displaying many of their merits. And even in his early Ukrainian stories Gogol was derivative in a number of ways. The cyclical structure and the 'evenings' of the title were both contemporary fashions; much of the specifically Little Russian material was supplied, at his request in letters home, by members of his family rather than by his own observation; and the elements of the supernatural that run through the two volumes (and continue in the fourth and last tale of *Mirgorod*, the spurious folk legend 'Viy') are reminiscent of other contemporary works now largely – and justly – forgotten. Vladimir Nabokov's comments on Russian literature can be idiosyncratic, yet he was perhaps correct in suggesting that these early writings reveal little of the brilliance to come.

But just as the Petersburg tales began to show fully the creative genius of Gogol's mind, so too did the Little Russian pieces from the same years indicate how he was to move on from the restrictive confines of formulaic writing, where he found the conventions hard to follow and where he was prevented from expressing his own imaginative power. This is not to say that Gogol suddenly gave up using any pre-existing literary framework for his writing. The full title of 'The Squabble' – 'The Tale of How Ivan Ivanovich Fell Out with Ivan Nikiforovich' – immediately calls to mind the titles of many eighteenth-century didactic tales as well as the historical chronicles of medieval Russia, while the narrative voice of 'Olde-Worlde Landowners' has a discernibly Sentimental ring to it. The difference was that Gogol had now begun to use literary sources more creatively, not attempting to write, say, a

Sentimental tale, but rather adopting some of the conventions of such tales as a starting-point for his own original, comic exploration of his subject matter.

Where Gogol's St Petersburg was a city of dreams, of phantoms and of madness, his Little Russia provides a landscape dominated by things, objects that are at times all-too material. The theme of acquisition was one that became increasingly important in Gogol's writing. In 'The Greatcoat', for example, a minor civil servant achieves a degree of humanity only when he purchases a new coat, but as a result is eventually punished, while in the uncompleted epic *Dead Souls* this materialism becomes linked with the seemingly antithetical theme of the phantom, when the anti-heroic protagonist seeks to acquire non-existent serfs to further a financial scam. The innocent beginnings of what in Gogol's cosmology is an ultimately excessive and sinful concern with the material world are there to be seen in the lifestyle of the olde-worlde landowners, revolving exclusively around items of food and drink. In an ironic reworking of the myth of Philemon and Baucis it is symptomatic that the end of the old couple's distorted Arcadian idyll is signalled by the loss of a possession. 'The Squabble' is a tale of the terrible effects of an unrequited desire for the acquisition of a superfluous object on relations between two previously friendly neighbours, and can be seen as a commentary not only on human nature, but also on international affairs. And even in the slightest of these stories, 'The Carriage', the object of the title is supposed, rather like the eponymous greatcoat, to afford its owner status as well as possible financial gain, yet proprietorial pride turns out to be the source of eventual disaster.

In the detail of these stories too, it is objects that in many instances stand out. The singing doors of 'Olde-Worlde

Landowners', the soldiers' moustaches in 'The Carriage', the mayor's leg in 'The Squabble' are all memorable, thanks to the attention afforded them by the idiosyncratic narrative voices. Indeed, it is typical of Gogol's narratives for things that the reader might think worthy merely of passing mention to gain much greater stature through the unexpected wealth of detail given about them. Such digressive passages vary in length and may be lyrical, grotesque, or even presented in a mixture of styles, but all are striking for their ingenuity and originality, and can perhaps be seen as a stylistic expression of the unpredictability of the Gogolian universe. For if these stories are set in a largely objective world, the presence of another plane of existence can nonetheless often be sensed near at hand: the intrusion of the wild woodland on the life of the paragon of housekeeping in 'Olde-Worlde Landowners' and the intervention of a pig in the conduct of justice in 'The Squabble' are prime examples, and it is no matter of chance that the Devil is mentioned so frequently in Gogol's stories. The writer was a profoundly religious man whose final tragedy was that he could not reconcile the nature of his creative gift with what he regarded as his spiritual duty. Thus his masterpiece *Dead Souls* was meant to trace the regeneration of a sinful soul in a trilogy inspired by Dante, but Gogol was able to complete to his own artistic satisfaction only the first part of the project, the equivalent of Dante's *Inferno*.

It is appropriately paradoxical and ironic that a man whose ultimate artistic aim was to complete a great project of national spiritual significance should have been blessed with a talent for the evocative depiction of the insignificant (rickety houses, pictures on a wall, an old coat) and even mere parts of a whole (buttons, moustaches, legs). Of course, the stories at the heart of 'The Squabble' and 'The Carriage' are amusing in themselves, but, as always with comedy, it is the way Gogol tells them that is most striking, and it is his comic vision that is able to transform 'Olde-Worlde Landowners', a Sentimental tale of death and loss, into what Pushkin described as 'a humorous, touching idyll which makes you laugh through tears of sorrow and emotion' – the deathbed conversation of mistress with housekeeper is a case in point. Gogol's humour feels, in fact, very modern, in that it often relies for its effect on elements of the grotesque and the absurd so familiar today. These features are also evident in the intermittent unevenness of Gogol's style, for the unpredictability already referred to is present even at the linguistic level of shifts in register from one sentence to the next.

In general, Gogol's interest for today's reader is assured by virtue of his affinities with influences on the modern cultural psyche as diverse as Franz Kafka and Monty Python, and it comes as no surprise that his work has been the subject of a critical monograph that adopted Freudian psychoanalysis as its chief tool. The world that Gogol depicted in these stories is that of nineteenth-century Little Russia, it is true, but in choosing as the setting for 'The Squabble' the Ukrainian town of Mirgorod, which in translation means Worldtown, he was arguably suggesting a far wider relevance for his vision.

– Hugh Aplin, 2002

The Squabble

or

The Tale of How Ivan Ivanovich Fell Out with Ivan Nikiforovich

I consider it my duty to forewarn the reader that the event described in this tale relates to a very distant time. Moreover, it is a complete invention. Mirgorod is now quite another place. The buildings are different; the puddle in the middle of the town dried up ages ago, and the dignitaries, the judge, the clerk of the court and the mayor are all respected and well-intentioned men.

CHAPTER ONE

Ivan Ivanovich and Ivan Nikiforovich

Ivan Ivanovich has a glorious coat! Quite excellent! And what lambskins! Damn it all, what lambskins! They're grey-blue with a touch of frost! God knows how much I'd bet that nobody can be found with any like them! Just look at them, for God's sake, especially if he starts talking to someone, look at them from the side; what a feast for the eye. Indescribable: velvet! silver! fire! My God, good Lord! Nicholas the Miracle-Worker, God's saint! why, oh why haven't I got such a coat! He had it made even before Agafya Fedoseyevna travelled to Kiev. Do you know Agafya Fedoseyevna, the one that bit off the district assessor's ear?

Ivan Ivanovich is a splendid man! What a house he has in Mirgorod! It's surrounded on all four sides by a projecting roof supported by oak pillars, and there are benches everywhere on this veranda. When it gets too hot Ivan Ivanovich sheds both his coat and his trousers, keeps on just his undershirt, and relaxes on the veranda, keeping an eye on what's happening in the yard and in the street. What apple and pear trees he has right outside the windows! You only have to open the window for the branches to burst into the room. That's all at the front of the house, but you should take a look at what he's got in the garden! What hasn't he got there? Plum trees, black-cherry trees, red-cherry trees, all sorts of vegetables, sunflowers, cucumbers, melons, beans, even a threshing-floor and a smithy.

Ivan Ivanovich is a splendid man! He's very fond of melons. They're his favourite food. No sooner has he eaten lunch and come out onto the veranda wearing just his undershirt, than he orders Gapka to bring him two melons. But he cuts them up himself, collects the seeds into a special paper packet and starts eating. Then he orders Gapka to bring him the inkstand and, with his very own hand, he makes an inscription on the paper packet containing the seeds: 'this melon was eaten on such-and-such a date'. And if there was any guest in attendance: 'with the participation of so-and-so'. The late judge of Mirgorod was always full of admiration when looking at Ivan Ivanovich's house. Yes, it's not a bad little place at all. I like the fact that it has entrances big and small built onto it on all sides, so that if you glance at it from a distance, you can see only roofs, piled one on top of another, which looks a lot like a plate filled with pancakes, or, even better, like fungi growing on a tree. Anyway, the roofs are all covered with bog-rushes; a willow, an oak and two apple trees have their spreading branches leaning on them. Between the trees little windows with carved whitewashed shutters can be glimpsed and they even look out quickly into the street.

Ivan Ivanovich is a splendid man! Even the commissioner in Poltava knows him! Dorosh Tarasovich Pukhivochka always drops in on him whenever he's travelling from Khorol. And the archpriest Father Pyotr that lives in Koliberda always says, whenever he has half a dozen or so guests gathered, that he doesn't know anybody who does his Christian duty or lives his life so well as Ivan Ivanovich does. God, how time flies! Even then more than ten years had passed since he lost his wife. He had no children. Gapka has children and they often run around in the yard. Ivan Ivanovich always gives each of them either a bagel, or a piece of melon, or a pear. His Gapka has the keys to the storerooms and cellars; but the keys to the big chest that stands in his bedroom and to the middle storeroom Ivan Ivanovich keeps to himself, and he doesn't like letting anybody in there. Gapka, who's a strapping girl, goes around in a loose skirt with fresh calves and cheeks. And what a devout man Ivan Ivanovich is! Every Sunday he puts on his coat and goes to church. Ivan Ivanovich ascends the steps, bows to all sides, then usually finds himself a place in the choir and sings along nicely in his bass voice. And when the service is over, Ivan Ivanovich just can't restrain himself from going around all the beggars. Perhaps he wouldn't have wanted to do something so boring, had it not been for his innate kindness prompting him to do so.

'Hello, pauper!' he usually said, when he had found the most crippled woman, wearing tattered clothing sewn out of patches. 'Where are you from, my poor woman?' – 'I've come from the farm, master. It's been three days I've had nothing to drink or eat, driven out by my own children.' – 'So why have you come here, you poor thing?' – 'Why, master, to beg for alms. Perhaps someone might give me just a little to buy bread.' – 'Hm! Would you really like some bread, then?' Ivan Ivanovich usually asked. – 'Of course I would! I'm hungry as a dog.' – 'Hm!' Ivan Ivanovich usually replied: 'Perhaps you'd like some meat as well?' – 'Anything your kindness allows, I'll be content with it all.' – 'Hm! Would meat be better than bread, then?' – 'How's a hungry person to decide? Anything you can spare, it'll all be good.' With this the old woman usually stretched out her hand. 'Well, may God be with you,' said Ivan Ivanovich. 'What are you standing here for? I'm not hitting you, am I?' And after putting similar questions to a second, then a third, he finally returns home, or drops in on his neighbour, Ivan Nikiforovich, or the judge, or the mayor, to drink a glass of vodka. Ivan Ivanovich really loves it when somebody gives him a present or a treat. He likes that a lot.

Ivan Nikiforovich is a very good man as well. His yard is

next to Ivan Ivanovich's yard. They are friends, such as the world has never produced. Anton Prokofyevich Pupopuz, who to this very day still wears the brown frock-coat with blue sleeves and dines with the judge on Sundays, used to say that Ivan Nikiforovich and Ivan Ivanovich had been roped together by the Devil himself. Wherever the one goes, the other goes too. Ivan Nikiforovich was never married. Although they sometimes used to say that he had been married, that was a downright lie. I know Ivan Nikiforovich very well, and I can say that he never even had any intention of marrying. Where does all this gossip come from? Because they tried to spread it about that Ivan Nikiforovich was born with a tail on his behind. But that invention is so absurd, and both vile and indecent, that I don't even consider it necessary to refute it before my enlightened readers, who are without any doubt aware that only witches, and very few of them too, have a tail on their behind, and they, incidentally, belong more to the female sex than the male.

Despite their great affection, these rare friends were not entirely similar to one another. You can learn about their characters best of all by comparison. Ivan Ivanovich has an unusual gift for speaking extremely pleasantly. Lord, how he can speak! The sensation can only be compared with when you're having your head deloused, or when someone runs a finger gently over your heel. You listen and listen – and you hang your head. How pleasant! Extremely pleasant! Like sleeping after a bath. Ivan Nikiforovich is, on the contrary, mostly silent, yet if he puts in a word, just hold on tight: he'll shave you closer than any razor. Ivan Ivanovich is tall and lean; Ivan Nikiforovich is a little shorter, yet expansive in girth. Ivan Ivanovich's head looks like a radish with the tail downwards; Ivan Nikiforovich's head is like a radish with the tail upwards.

Only after lunch does Ivan Ivanovich lie on the veranda wearing nothing but his undershirt, for in the evening he puts on his coat and goes out somewhere, either to the town shop, which he supplies with flour, or into the fields to catch quail. Ivan Nikiforovich lies on the porch all day long; if the day isn't too hot, he usually has his back in the sunshine and doesn't want to go out anywhere. If it occurs to him in the morning, he'll take a walk around the yard, inspect his holding, and then go back to rest. In former times he used to drop in on Ivan Ivanovich.

Ivan Ivanovich is an extremely delicate man and would never utter an indecent word in a respectable conversation, and would take offence at once if he heard one. Ivan Nikiforovich is sometimes unguarded; at such times Ivan Ivanovich rises from his seat and says: 'Enough, enough, Ivan Nikiforovich; better to get out into the sun quickly, than utter such impious words.'

Ivan Ivanovich gets very angry if a fly finds its way into his borsch; at such times he loses control of himself, throws plates around and his host catches it as well. Ivan Nikiforovich is extremely fond of bathing, and when he's sitting up to his neck in water, he orders the table and samovar to be placed in the water too, and he really likes drinking tea in the cool like that. Ivan Ivanovich shaves his beard twice a week, Ivan Nikiforovich once. Ivan Ivanovich is extremely curious. God forbid that anybody should start telling him something and then not finish! If he's ever unhappy with anything, he lets it be seen straight away. From Ivan Nikiforovich's appearance it's extremely hard to ascertain whether he's content or angry; even when he's pleased about something he won't show it. Ivan Ivanovich is somewhat fearful in character. Ivan Nikiforovich, on the contrary, has baggy trousers with such deep folds that if you were to inflate them, then the entire yard with its barns and buildings could fit inside them.

Ivan Ivanovich has large expressive eyes the colour of tobacco and a mouth somewhat similar to the letter V; Ivan Nikiforovich has small, yellowish eyes, which completely disappear between his thick eyebrows and his plump cheeks, and a nose in the shape of a ripe plum. If Ivan Ivanovich regales you with snuff, he will always lick the lid of the snuffbox first with his tongue, then flick it with his finger, and then, proffering it, will say, if you're acquainted with him, 'Dare I beg you, my good sir, to do me the favour?', or if you're not acquainted, then, 'Dare I beg you, my good sir, without having the honour to know your rank, first name and patronymic, to do me the favour?', whereas Ivan Nikiforovich passes his snuff-horn directly into your hands and adds simply, 'Help yourself!'

Both Ivan Ivanovich and Ivan Nikiforovich dislike fleas immensely; and for that reason neither Ivan Ivanovich nor Ivan Nikiforovich will ever let a Jewish salesman go by without purchasing from him various little jars of elixir to guard against these insects, having first given him a good dressing down for confessing the Jewish faith.

Anyway, in spite of certain dissimilarities, both Ivan Ivanovich and Ivan Nikiforovich are splendid people.

CHAPTER TWO

*From which can be learned what Ivan Ivanovich took a fancy
to, what was the topic of conversation between Ivan Ivanovich
and Ivan Nikiforovich, and what was its outcome*

One morning in the month of July, Ivan Ivanovich was lying
on his veranda. The day was hot and the air was dry with
undulating currents. Ivan Ivanovich had already managed to
spend some time in the countryside with the mowers, and on
the farm, managed to question the peasant men and women he
had encountered about where they were from, where they
were going and why; he had worn himself out dreadfully and
lain down to take a rest. From a recumbent position he spent a
long time examining the storerooms, the yard, the sheds, the
chickens running around the yard, and thought to himself,
'My God, Lord above, what a master I am! What haven't I got?
Poultry, buildings, barns, all sorts of fancy stuff, distilled
liqueur vodka; pear trees and plum trees in the orchard;
poppies, cabbage and peas in the kitchen garden… What
haven't I got yet?… That's what I'd like to know, what haven't
I got?'

Asking himself this profound question, Ivan Ivanovich fell
into thought; but meanwhile his eyes had sought out some
new objects, they'd stepped over the fence into Ivan
Nikiforovich's yard and involuntarily busied themselves with a
curious spectacle. A skinny peasant woman was bringing out a
succession of long-unused items of clothing and hanging them
up on a line to air. Soon an old uniform jacket with threadbare
cuffs stretched its sleeves out to embrace a brocade blouse,
poking out beyond them was a nobleman's coat with buttons
bearing a coat of arms and with a moth-eaten collar, and white

kerseymere trousers with stains on them, which once used to be pulled onto Ivan Nikiforovich's legs but which you'd now be lucky to pull onto his toes.

Soon another pair was hung up beyond them in the shape of the letter pi. Then came a blue padded Cossack jacket which Ivan Nikiforovich had had made for himself some twenty years before when he was preparing to join the militia and was about to grow whiskers. To these was finally added a sword which resembled a spire sticking up into the air. Next there revolved the tails of something resembling a grass-green caftan, with brass buttons the size of five-kopek coins. From behind the tails there peeped a waistcoat, edged with gold braid and with a low neck at the front. The waistcoat was soon hidden by his late grandmother's old skirt, with pockets into each of which you could fit a watermelon.

Mixed together, all this made up a very engaging spectacle for Ivan Ivanovich, while the rays of the sun, catching in places a blue or green sleeve, a red cuff or a piece of gold brocade, or playing on the sword-spire, made it into something extra-ordinary, like the nativity play puppet-show that itinerant rogues take around the farms. Especially when the crowd of people, pressing close together, gaze at King Herod in his golden crown, or at Anton, leading the nanny-goat; behind the puppet-show a fiddle screeches; a gypsy beats a rhythm on his own lips in place of a drum, while the sun goes down and the fresh cool of the southern night imperceptibly squeezes tighter to the fresh shoulders and breasts of the buxom farm-girls.

Soon the old woman clambered out of the storeroom, wheezing under the weight of an ancient saddle with ragged stirrups, rubbed leather pistol holsters, a saddle-cloth that had once been scarlet, gold stitching and horse brasses. 'What a stupid woman!' thought Ivan Ivanovich. 'She'll be dragging

Ivan Nikiforovich himself out to air next!' And so it was; Ivan Ivanovich was not entirely wrong in his conjecture. Five minutes later Ivan Nikiforovich's baggy nankeen trousers reared up and took over almost half the yard. After that she brought out a hat and gun as well. 'What can this mean?' thought Ivan Ivanovich. 'I've never seen Ivan Nikiforovich with a gun. What's he doing? He doesn't shoot, but he keeps a gun! What does he need that for? And it's a glorious little thing! I've wanted to get myself one like that for ages. I really fancy having that nice little gun; I like having a bit of fun with a nice little gun. Hey, you, peasant woman!' shouted Ivan Ivanovich, beckoning with his finger.

The old woman came up to the fence.

'What's that you've got there, granny?'

'You can see for yourself, it's a gun.'

'What sort of gun?'

'How should I know what sort! If it was mine, perhaps I'd know what it was made of. But it's the master's.'

Ivan Ivanovich got up and began examining the gun from all sides, and quite forgot to give the old woman a reprimand for hanging it out to air with the sword.

'I'd have thought it's iron,' continued the old woman.

'Hm! Iron. Why should it be iron?' said Ivan Ivanovich to himself. 'And has the master had it long?'

'Perhaps he has, yes.'

'It's a nice little thing,' continued Ivan Ivanovich. 'I'll ask him to give it to me. What's he going to do with it! Or I'll exchange something for it. Well, granny, is the master in?'

'He is.'

'What's he doing? Having a lie down?'

'That's right.'

'Very good. I'll come and see him.'

Ivan Ivanovich got dressed, picked up his knotty stick to beat off the dogs, because in Mirgorod you meet far more of them in the street than you do people, and set off.

Although Ivan Nikiforovich's yard was next to Ivan Ivanovich's yard and you could clamber from one to the other across the wattle fencing, Ivan Ivanovich nonetheless went via the street. From the street you needed to cross into an alleyway, which was so narrow that if two one-horse carriages happened to meet in it, they would be unable to pass and would remain in this position until someone grabbed hold of the rear wheels and dragged them, each in opposite directions, out into the street, and the pedestrian would be adorned, as if with flowers, with the burdock growing by the fence on both sides. Ivan Ivanovich's shed looked out onto this alleyway from one side; from the other, Ivan Nikiforovich's barn, gates and dovecot.

Ivan Ivanovich went up to the gates and began rattling at the latch. From within there came the barking of dogs; but the motley pack soon ran back, wagging their tails, when they saw that this was a familiar face. Ivan Ivanovich crossed the yard, where the eye was struck by the Indian doves, fed by Ivan Nikiforovich's very own hand, the rinds of watermelons and melons, in places some herbage, in others a broken wheel or a hoop from a barrel, or a little boy lying around in a dirty shirt – a picture beloved of artists! The shade from the clothes that had been hung out covered almost the entire yard and lent it a certain coolness. The peasant woman greeted him with a bow and remained gawping where she stood. In front of the house was a pretty little porch with an overhanging roof supported by two oak pillars – an unreliable defence against the sun, which doesn't joke in Little Russia at this time of the year and covers the pedestrian in hot sweat from head to toe. From this can be seen the strength of Ivan Ivanovich's desire to acquire an essential item, that he should have resolved to go out at such an hour, betraying even his constant practice of going for a walk only in the evening.

The room into which Ivan Ivanovich stepped was completely dark because the shutters were closed, and the ray of sunlight passing through a hole that had been made in a shutter assumed the colours of the rainbow and, striking the wall opposite, drew upon it a variegated landscape of bog-rush roofs, trees and the clothing hanging out in the yard, only all in an inverted form. Because of this the whole room was lent a wondrous twilight.

'God help me!' said Ivan Ivanovich.

'Ah, hello, Ivan Ivanovich!' replied a voice from the corner of the room. Only then did Ivan Ivanovich notice Ivan Nikiforovich lying on a rug spread out on the floor. 'Excuse my being naked in front of you.' Ivan Nikiforovich lay there without a stitch on, without even his undershirt.

'Never mind. Have you had a sleep today, Ivan Nikiforovich?'

'I have. And have you had a sleep, Ivan Ivanovich?'

'I have.'

'And now have you just got up?'

'Have I just got up now? May the Lord be with you, Ivan Nikiforovich! How is it possible to sleep all this time! I've just come back from the farm. The rye along the way looks splendid! Delightful! And the hay is so tall, so soft and lush!'

'Gorpina!' called Ivan Nikiforovich. 'Bring Ivan Ivanovich some vodka and some pies with sour cream.'

'Good weather today.'

'Don't praise it, Ivan Ivanovich. The Devil take it! You can't escape the heat anywhere.'

'And of course you have to bring the Devil into it. Hey, Ivan Nikiforovich! You'll remember what I say when it's already too late: you'll catch it in the next world for your impious words.'

'How have I offended you, Ivan Ivanovich? I never touched upon your father or mother. I don't know how I've offended you.'

'All right, Ivan Nikiforovich, that's enough now.'

'I swear to God, I never offended you, Ivan Ivanovich!'

'It's strange, but the quail are still not responding to the pipe.'

'As you wish, you can think what you like, only I did nothing to offend you.'

'I don't know why they don't respond,' said Ivan Ivanovich, as if not listening to Ivan Nikiforovich. 'Perhaps the time isn't ripe yet, only it would seem to be the right time.'

'You say the rye's looking good.'

'The rye's delightful, delightful!' After which a silence ensued.

'Why is it, Ivan Nikiforovich, you're hanging clothes out?' said Ivan Ivanovich finally.

'Because perfectly good clothes, almost new, have been allowed to rot by that damned woman. So now I'm airing them, the cloth's good quality, excellent stuff, just turn them inside out and you can wear them again.'

'I've taken a liking to one little thing out there, Ivan Nikiforovich.'

'What's that?'

'Tell me, please, what do you need that gun for, the one put out to air along with the clothes?' At this point Ivan Ivanovich proffered some snuff. 'Dare I beg you to do me the favour?'

'Never mind, help yourself! I'll take my own!' With this Ivan Nikiforovich fumbled around himself and found his horn.

'What a stupid woman, so she hung the gun out there too! It's good snuff that Jew in Sorochintsy makes. I don't know what he puts in it, but it's so aromatic! It's a bit like costmary. Here, take some, chew on it a while. It is like costmary, isn't it? Take some, help yourself!'

'Do please tell me, Ivan Nikiforovich, I'm still talking about the gun, what are you going to do with it? After all, you don't need it.'

'What do you mean, I don't need it? And what if I went shooting?'

'The Lord be with you, Ivan Nikiforovich, and when will you be going shooting? Only after the second coming, perhaps. So far as I know and others can remember, you've yet to kill a single duck, and what's more, the Lord God didn't give you the sort of nature to go shooting. You've an imposing bearing and figure. How could you go dragging around the marshes when that clothing of yours that can't decently be named in any language is still airing even now, so what then? No, you need to have peace and quiet.' (Ivan Ivanovich, as mentioned above, spoke in an extraordinarily picturesque manner when he needed to persuade anybody. How he spoke! God, how he spoke!) 'Yes, so you need decent behaviour. Listen, give it to me!'

'How can I? It's an expensive gun. You won't find guns like that anywhere nowadays. It was when I was going to join the militia I bought it from a Turk. And now I'm supposed to give it away all of a sudden! How can I? It's an essential thing.'

'And what is it essential for?'

'What do you mean, what for? And when the house is attacked by brigands?… And you say it's not essential. The Good Lord be praised, I'm at peace now and not afraid of anyone. And why? Because I know I have the gun standing in the storeroom.'

'It's a good gun! But, Ivan Nikiforovich, the lock's ruined.'

'So what if it is ruined? It can be mended. It only needs to have some hempseed oil put on to stop it rusting.'

'I can't see any amicable disposition towards me in what you say, Ivan Nikiforovich. You don't want to do anything for me as a mark of friendship.'

'How can you say that I don't show you any friendship, Ivan Ivanovich? You should be ashamed of yourself! Your oxen graze on my land, and not once have I touched them. When you go to Poltava you always ask for my carriage, and what? Have I ever refused? Your kids climb over the fence into my yard to play with my dogs, and I say nothing: let them play, as long as they don't touch anything! Let them play!'

'As you don't want to give it to me, perhaps we could do a swap.'

'And what will you give me for it?' Saying this, Ivan Nikiforovich raised himself onto one elbow and looked at Ivan Ivanovich.

'I'll give you the brown pig for it, the one I fattened up in the sty. It's a marvellous pig! You see if it doesn't have piglets for you next year.'

'Ivan Ivanovich, I don't know how you can say this. What do I need your pig for? Only to hold a wake for the Devil.'

'Again! You just can't get by without the Devil! It's a sin, I swear to God it is, Ivan Nikiforovich!'

'But really, Ivan Ivanovich, how is it you can give the Devil knows what, a pig, in exchange for a gun.'

'And why is it the Devil knows what, Ivan Nikiforovich?'

'What do you mean? Judge properly for yourself: a gun – that's something you know; but the Devil knows what a pig is. If it weren't you talking, I might take that as offensive towards me.'

'And what have you seen that's wrong with the pig?'

'But really, who do you take me for? That a pig…'

'Calm down, calm down! I've finished now… You keep your gun, let it rot and rust away, standing in the corner of the storeroom – I don't want to talk about it any more.'

After this a silence ensued.

'They say,' began Ivan Ivanovich, 'that three kings have declared war on our tsar.'

'Yes, Pyotr Fyodorovich was telling me; what is it, this war, what's it about?'

'You can't tell for sure, Ivan Nikiforovich, what it's over. I suppose the kings want us all to adopt the Turkish faith.'

'Just look at that, the idiots, what a thing to want!' said Ivan Nikiforovich, raising his head a little.

'There, you see, and our tsar has declared war on them for that. No, he says, you adopt the Christian faith!'

'Well then, our boys will beat them, won't they, Ivan Ivanovich?'

'They will. So, Ivan Nikiforovich, you don't want to swap your nice little gun?'

'I find it strange, Ivan Ivanovich. I thought you were a man known for his educated ways, yet you talk like a stupid youngster. That I should be such an idiot…'

'Calm down, calm down. Forget about it! Let it drop. I won't say another word!…'

At this point refreshments were brought.

Ivan Ivanovich drank a glass of vodka and ate a pie with sour cream. 'Listen, Ivan Nikiforovich, besides the pig I'll give you two sacks of oats; after all, you didn't sow any oats. You'll need to buy oats this year anyway.'

'I swear to God, Ivan Ivanovich, the only way to talk to you is on a bellyful of peas.' (This was nothing, Ivan Nikiforovich uses expressions worse than that.) 'Where does anybody swap a gun for two sacks of oats? I don't suppose you'll put up your coat.'

'But you've forgotten, Ivan Nikiforovich, I'm giving you a pig as well.'

'What's that! Two sacks of oats and a pig for the gun?'

'Well, isn't that enough?'

'For the gun?'

'Of course it's for the gun.'

'Two sacks for the gun?'

'Not two empty sacks, but sacks of oats; and have you forgotten the pig?'

'You can go and kiss your pig, or if you'd prefer it, then the Devil!'

'Oh, you're so touchy! You'll see, in the other world you'll have your tongue studded with hot needles for such blasphemous words. After a conversation with you, people need to wash their hands and face, and fumigate themselves.'

'Allow me, Ivan Ivanovich. A gun is a noble thing, the most curious amusement, and, what's more, a nice decoration in a room…'

'You, Ivan Nikiforovich, are fussing over your gun like a *bear with a sore head*,' said Ivan Ivanovich in annoyance, because he was truly beginning to get angry now.

'And you, Ivan Ivanovich, are a real *goose*.'

If Ivan Nikiforovich had not used this word they would have argued with one another and parted, as always, as friends; but now something entirely different took place. Ivan Ivanovich flared up.

'What was that you said, Ivan Nikiforovich?' he asked in a raised voice.

'I said that you were like a goose, Ivan Ivanovich!'

'How dare you, sir, forget both decency and respect for a man's rank and family, and dishonour him with such an abusive name?'

'What's abusive in that? And really, why are you waving your arms about like that, Ivan Ivanovich?'

'I repeat, how dare you, contrary to all the proprieties, call me a goose.'

'A plague on your head, Ivan Ivanovich! What is it you're cackling about so?'

Ivan Ivanovich could no longer control himself; his lips were trembling; his mouth had altered its normal V shape, and become like an O; he was blinking his eyes so, it was frightening. This was extremely rare for Ivan Ivanovich. He had to be made very angry for this. 'Right then, I declare to you,' pronounced Ivan Ivanovich, 'that I wish to hear from you no more.'

'There's a great loss! I swear to God, I won't be crying over that!' replied Ivan Nikiforovich. He was lying, lying, I swear to God, he was lying! This was very upsetting for him.

'I shan't set foot in your house.'

'Ahem, ahem!' said Ivan Nikiforovich, so upset, he didn't know himself what to do, and contrary to his custom he got to his feet. 'Hey, old woman, lad!' At this there appeared from behind the doors that same skinny peasant woman and a short boy, tangled up in a long, wide frock-coat. 'Take Ivan Ivanovich by the arms and show him outside!'

'What? A nobleman?' cried Ivan Ivanovich, with a sense of dignity and indignation. 'Just you dare! One step closer and I'll annihilate you and your stupid master! Even a raven won't find the spot where you lie!' (Ivan Ivanovich spoke with unusual power when his soul was stirred.) The group as a whole presented a powerful picture: Ivan Nikiforovich, who stood in the middle of the room in all his beauty without any adornment; the woman, her mouth agape and her face displaying the most senseless, terror-stricken expression; Ivan Ivanovich with his arm raised aloft in the way Roman tribunes were depicted... This was an extraordinary moment! A magnificent spectacle! And yet there was just the one spectator: this was the boy in the immeasurable frock-coat, who stood quite calmly cleaning his nose out with his finger.

Finally Ivan Ivanovich took hold of his hat. 'You're behaving very well, Ivan Nikiforovich! Splendidly! I'll remind you of this.'

'Be off, Ivan Ivanovich, be off! And see that I don't come across you: otherwise, Ivan Ivanovich, I'll smash your whole face in!'

'Take this in return, Ivan Nikiforovich!' replied Ivan Ivanovich, making a rude gesture with his hand and slamming the door behind him; with a squeal it began to creak and opened once again. Ivan Nikiforovich appeared in the doorway, wanting to say something more, but Ivan Ivanovich was already flying out of the yard without a backward glance.

CHAPTER THREE

What happened after the argument between Ivan Ivanovich and Ivan Nikiforovich

And so two respected men, the honour and adornment of Mirgorod, fell out! And over what? Over nonsense, over a goose. They didn't want to see one another; they broke off all links, whereas previously they were known as the most inseparable friends! Every day Ivan Ivanovich and Ivan Nikiforovich used to send to enquire after one another's health, and often conversed with one another from their balconies, and made such pleasant speeches to one another that it did your heart good to listen to them. On Sundays Ivan Ivanovich in his woollen coat and Ivan Nikiforovich in his yellowish-brown nankeen coat with the pleated skirt used to set out all but arm-in-arm with one another for church. And if Ivan Ivanovich, who had extremely sharp eyes, was the first to notice a puddle or some dirt in the middle of the road, such as you sometimes find in Mirgorod, then he would always say to Ivan Nikiforovich, 'Be careful, don't step there, for it's not nice there.' Ivan Nikiforovich for his part also displayed the most touching signs of friendship, and no matter how far away he was standing, he always used to stretch out to Ivan Ivanovich the hand holding his horn, adding as he did so, 'Help yourself!' And what splendid properties they both have!... And these two friends... When I heard about it, I was thunderstruck! For a long time I didn't want to believe it. Good God! Ivan Ivanovich has fallen out with Ivan Nikiforovich! Such worthy men! What is there that's lasting now in this world?

When Ivan Ivanovich arrived home, he was greatly agitated

for a long time. He used to drop in first of all at the stables to see if the filly was eating the hay (Ivan Ivanovich's filly is light brown with a dark mane and tail and a bald patch on the forehead – she's a very nice horse); then he would feed the turkeys and piglets from his own hands; and only then did he go to his rooms, where he would either make wooden utensils (he's very skilled, no less so than a turner, at making various things out of wood), or read a book printed by Lyuby, Gary and Popov (its title Ivan Ivanovich doesn't remember because his girl tore off the top part of the title-page ages ago to amuse a child), or else relax on his veranda. But now he didn't take up any of his constant pastimes. Instead, when he encountered Gapka, he began to scold her for wandering around doing nothing, although she was actually lugging groats into the kitchen; he threw a stick at the cockerel which had come to the porch for its customary hand-out; and when a filthy little boy in a ripped shirt ran up to him and shouted, 'Daddy, Daddy, give me some gingerbread!' he so frightened him with his threats and the stamping of his feet that the terrified child ran off God knows where.

Finally, however, he recovered his senses and began getting on with his regular business. He had his dinner late, and it was already almost evening when he lay down for a rest on the veranda. The tasty borsch with pigeons which Gapka had made had completely driven the morning's event out of his head. Ivan Ivanovich again began inspecting his property with pleasure. Finally he halted his eyes on his neighbour's yard and said to himself: 'I've not been to see Ivan Nikiforovich today. I'll pay him a visit.' Saying this, Ivan Ivanovich took up his stick and hat and set off into the street, but no sooner had he gone out of the gates than he remembered the quarrel, spat and went back again. Almost the identical movement took place in Ivan Nikiforovich's yard as well. Ivan Ivanovich saw the peasant woman putting her foot on the fence with the intention of climbing over into his yard, when suddenly Ivan Nikiforovich's voice was heard: 'Come back! Come back! There's no need!' However, Ivan Ivanovich got very bored. It might well have been the case that these worthy men would have made their peace on the very next day, had a particular occurrence in Ivan Nikiforovich's house not destroyed all hope and not added fuel to the fire of an enmity that was ready to die out.

In the evening of that same day Ivan Nikiforovich received a visit from Agafya Fedoseyevna. Agafya Fedoseyevna wasn't a relative of Ivan Nikiforovich's, nor his wife's sister, nor even his child's godmother. It would have seemed that there was absolutely no reason for her to visit him, and he wasn't too pleased to see her himself; however, she did pay him visits and would stay with him for weeks on end or sometimes even longer. Then she used to take away his keys and gather the entire household into her own hands. This was very unpleasant for Ivan Nikiforovich; surprisingly, however, he obeyed her like a child, and although at times he did try to argue, Agafya Fedoseyevna always had the upper hand.

I confess I don't understand why things are so arranged that women can take us by the nose just as deftly as they do a teapot by the handle? Either their hands are made that way, or our noses are good for nothing else. And despite the fact that Ivan Nikiforovich's nose was rather like a plum, still she grabbed him by this nose and led him behind her like a lapdog. With her about he even involuntarily changed his normal way of life: he didn't lie in the sun so long, and when he did it wasn't in the nude, but always wearing his shirt and baggy trousers, although Agafya Fedoseyevna didn't demand this at all. She wasn't one to stand on ceremony, and when Ivan Nikiforovich had a fever, she herself rubbed him down with her own hands from head to toe with turpentine and vinegar. Agafya Fedoseyevna wore a bonnet on her head, three warts on her nose and a coffee-coloured housecoat with little yellow flowers. Her figure as a whole resembled a cotton reel, and for that reason it was just as difficult to find her waist as it is to see your own nose without a mirror. Her legs were short and shaped on the model of two cushions. She gossiped, ate boiled beetroot in the mornings, and was really great at swearing – and while engaged in all these varied activities, her face never altered its expression for a single moment, which is a trick that usually only women can perform.

As soon as she arrived, everything was turned inside out. 'You, Ivan Nikiforovich, are not to make up with him and not to ask forgiveness – he wants to destroy you, he's that sort of man! You don't know him yet at all.' The damned woman whispered and whispered, with the effect that Ivan Nikiforovich didn't even want to hear of Ivan Ivanovich.

Everything took on a new look: if the neighbour's dog slipped into the yard, it was given a drubbing with anything that came to hand; the little kids who climbed over the fence went back screaming, with their shirts pulled up and the marks of a birching on their backs. Even the old peasant woman, when Ivan Ivanovich was about to try and ask her a question, did something so indecent that Ivan Ivanovich, being an extremely delicate man, spat and said only, 'What a nasty woman! Worse than her master!'

Finally, to add the final insult, the hateful neighbour constructed directly opposite him, in the spot where there was normally a gap in the fencing, a goose coop, as if with the specific intention of deepening the insult. This coop, so repellent for Ivan Ivanovich, was constructed with devilish speed – in a single day.

This aroused in Ivan Ivanovich malicious anger and a desire for revenge. He didn't give any appearance of distress, however, despite the fact that the coop even occupied a part of his land; but his heart was beating so hard that it was extremely difficult for him to maintain this calm exterior.

Thus did he spend the day. Then night fell… Oh, if I were a painter I should wondrously depict all the charm of the night! I should depict the whole of Mirgorod asleep; the countless immobile stars gazing down on it; the apparent silence resounding with the barking of dogs near and far; the lovelorn sexton hurrying past them and clambering over a fence with chivalric fearlessness; the white walls of the houses becoming whiter in the enveloping moonlight, the trees that shield them becoming darker, the shadow from the trees falling blacker, the flowers and the silent grass ever more fragrant, and the crickets, those indefatigable paladins of the night, amicably striking up their clicking songs from every corner.

I should depict how in one of these low, clay houses, tossing and turning in her lonely bed, a black-browed lady of the town with trembling young breasts dreams of a hussar's moustache and spurs, while the light of the moon laughs on her cheeks. I should depict the black shadow of a bat flashing along the white road as it settles on the white chimneys of the houses…

But scarcely should I be able to depict Ivan Ivanovich, who emerged that night with a saw in his hand. So many different emotions were written on his face! Softly, softly he stole up and clambered under the goose coop. Ivan Nikiforovich's dogs still knew nothing about the squabble between them and so allowed him as an old friend to approach the coop, which was entirely held on four oak pillars. Shuffling up to the nearest pillar, he set his saw to it and began sawing. The noise produced by the saw made him look around continually; but the thought of his grievance restored his pluck. The first pillar was sawn through; Ivan Ivanovich started on another. His eyes were burning and in terror could see nothing. Suddenly Ivan Ivanovich shrieked and froze: he thought he had seen a ghost; but he quickly recovered himself when he saw it was a goose poking its neck out towards him. Ivan Ivanovich spat indignantly and set about continuing his work. The second pillar too was sawn through; the edifice tottered. Ivan Ivanovich's heart began beating so dreadfully when he started on the third, that several times he stopped work; it was already more than half sawn through when suddenly the unsteady edifice lurched violently… Ivan Ivanovich barely managed to jump aside before it collapsed with a crash. Grabbing the saw, and in a dreadful fright, he ran home and threw himself onto his bed, without the courage even to glance out of the window at the consequences of his dreadful deed. It seemed to him that the whole of Ivan Nikiforovich's household had gathered: the old peasant woman, Ivan Nikiforovich, the boy in the endless frock-coat; and carrying staves, under the leadership of Agafya Fedoseyevna, they were all on their way to destroy and break up his house.

Ivan Ivanovich spent the whole of the following day as if in a fever. He kept imagining that his hateful neighbour would at the very least set fire to his house in revenge for this. And so he gave Gapka the command to keep on inspecting everywhere, in case dry straw had been laid down anywhere. Finally, to forestall Ivan Nikiforovich, he resolved to run on ahead, hare-like, and submit a petition against him to the Mirgorod district court. Of what it consisted can be learnt from the next chapter.

CHAPTER FOUR

*Concerning what took place in the courtroom
of the Mirgorod district court*

Mirgorod is a wonderful town! What buildings can one not find there! Beneath a straw roof, beneath a bog-rush roof, even beneath a wooden roof; to the right a street, to the left a street, everywhere splendid fencing; hops wind along it, pots hang on it, from behind it sunflowers show their sun-like heads, the poppies grow red and there are glimpses of fat pumpkins... Luxuriance! The fencing is always decorated with objects which make it even more picturesque, a hair-shirt spread wide, or a blouse, or baggy trousers. There is no thieving or swindling in Mirgorod, and for that reason anybody can hang up whatever he fancies. If you're approaching the square, you'll certainly stop for a while to admire the view; there is a puddle in it, an amazing puddle! The only one of its kind you have ever had the good fortune to see! It takes up almost the entire square! A splendid puddle! The buildings large and small that are gathered all around, and which can from a distance be taken for haycocks, wonder at its beauty.

Yet I am of the opinion that there is no better building than the district court. Whether it is of oak or birch is of no concern to me, but it has, kind sirs, eight windows! Eight windows in a row, looking directly onto the square and that watery expanse of which I have already spoken, and which the mayor calls a lake! It alone is painted the colour of granite: all the other buildings in Mirgorod are simply whitewashed. The roof upon it is entirely of wood, and might even have been painted with red paint if the oil that had been prepared for the purpose had not been consumed, flavoured with onions, by the clerks, something which happened, as if on purpose, during a fast, so the roof remained unpainted.

Onto the square juts the porch, on which there are often chickens running about, because there are almost always groats or something edible scattered on the porch; this isn't done on purpose, by the way, but is solely due to the carelessness of petitioners. The court is divided into two halves: in one is the *courtroom*, in the other are the *cells*. In the half where the courtroom is located there are two clean and whitewashed rooms: one ante-room for petitioners; in the other a table decorated with ink stains. On it a triangular prism bearing the decrees of Peter the Great. Four high-backed oak chairs; along the walls beaten iron chests in which were kept bundles of court records. On one of these chests there stood at that time a clean, waxed boot. Work had already begun in the courtroom early in the morning. The judge, quite a portly man, albeit somewhat slimmer than Ivan Nikiforovich, with a kind face, wearing a greasy dressing-gown and with a pipe and a cup of tea, was talking with the clerk of the court. The judge's lips were situated right underneath his nose, and for that reason his nose could sniff the upper lip to its heart's content. This upper lip served him in lieu of a snuffbox, because the snuff addressed to the nose was almost always sprinkled over it. And so the judge was talking with the clerk of the court. A barefooted girl stood to one side holding a tray of cups.

At the end of the table the secretary was reading out the verdict of a case, but in such a monotonous and mournful tone that the defendant himself would have fallen asleep while listening. The judge would without doubt have been the first to do so, if he had not meanwhile embarked upon an interest-ing conversation.

'I tried to find out specifically,' the judge was saying, as he sipped his tea from a cup that had already cooled, 'what method can be used to make them sing well. I had a fine thrush a couple of years ago, and what happened? All of a sudden it went completely wrong. Began singing God knows what. The longer it went on, the worse it became; it began singing with a burr, wheezing – a complete waste of space! And all for no reason, you see! This is why it happens: a swelling forms under the throat, smaller than a pea. This little swelling just needs to be pierced with a needle. Zakhar Prokofyevich taught me how, and, if you like, I'll tell you just how it came about: I arrive at his place…'

'Demyan Demyanovich, do you want me to read another?' interjected the secretary, who had finished his reading some minutes before.

'Oh, have you already finished? Just imagine, so quickly! I didn't even hear a thing! Where is it then? Give it here and I'll sign it. What else have you got there?'

'The case of the Cossack Bokitko and the stolen cow.'

'Very well, read on! Yes, so I arrive at his place… I can even give you details of how he entertained me. Cured fillet of sturgeon was served with the vodka, just the one! Yes, not like our sturgeon,' and at this the judge clicked his tongue and smiled, whereupon his nose sniffed at its permanent snuffbox, 'the stuff our Mirgorod grocer's treats us to. I didn't eat any herring, because, as you know yourself, it gives me heartburn in the pit of the stomach. But I tried some caviar – splendid caviar! It can't be denied, excellent! Then I drank some peach vodka infused with centaury. There was saffron vodka too; but as you know yourself, I don't drink saffron vodka. It's a very good thing, you see, to excite your appetite, as they say, in advance, and then after that to complete… Ah! Here's a sight for sore eyes…' cried the judge suddenly, seeing Ivan Ivanovich coming in.

'God help you! I wish you good health!' announced Ivan Ivanovich, bowing to all sides with the pleasantness characteristic of him alone. My God, how he could charm everyone with his manner! Nowhere have I seen such delicacy. He was very well aware of his own dignity, and therefore regarded universal respect as his due. The judge himself offered Ivan Ivanovich a chair, and his nose drew up all the snuff from his upper lip, which was always a sign of great pleasure in him.

'What refreshment can we offer you, Ivan Ivanovich?' he asked. 'Would you like a cup of tea?'

'I'm most grateful, but no,' Ivan Ivanovich replied, bowed and sat down.

'Do be so kind, just a little cup!' repeated the judge.

'Thank you, no. I'm quite content with your hospitality!' Ivan Ivanovich replied, bowed and sat down.

'Just the one cup,' repeated the judge.

'No, don't trouble yourself, Demyan Demyanovich!' With this Ivan Ivanovich bowed and sat down.

'A little cup?'

'As you say, then, just a little cup!' pronounced Ivan Ivanovich, and reached his hand out to the tray.

Lord God! What an abyss of delicacy a man can have! It's impossible to relate what a pleasant impression such actions make!

'Would you like another cup?'

'I'm humbly grateful,' replied Ivan Ivanovich, placing his upturned cup on the tray and bowing.

'Do us the favour, Ivan Ivanovich!'

'I can't. I'm most grateful.' With this Ivan Ivanovich bowed and sat down.

'Ivan Ivanovich, in token of friendship, one little cup!'

'No, I'm most obliged for the refreshment.' Saying this, Ivan Ivanovich bowed and sat down.

'Just a little cup! One little cup!'

Ivan Ivanovich reached out his hand to the tray and took a cup.

Damn it all! How does a man manage, have the presence to maintain such dignity!

'Demyan Demyanovich,' said Ivan Ivanovich, drinking down the last mouthful, 'I have an essential matter for you. I'm serving a writ.' With this Ivan Ivanovich set down his cup and took out of his pocket a sheet of stamped paper with writing on it: 'A writ on my enemy, my sworn enemy.'

'And who's that?'

'Ivan Nikiforovich Dovgochkhun.'

At these words the judge almost fell off his chair. 'What are you saying?' he uttered, clasping his hands together. 'Ivan Ivanovich! Is it you?'

'You can see for yourself that it's me.'

'May the Lord and all his saints be with you! What? You? Ivan Ivanovich? You've become the enemy of Ivan Nikiforovich! Is it your lips speaking? Say it again! Is somebody hiding behind you and speaking instead of you?…'

'What's so incredible about it? I can't stand the sight of him; he gave me mortal offence, insulted my honour.'

'Most Holy Trinity! How am I to reassure my mother now? Every day, as soon as my sister and I have a row, the old woman says, "Children, you live together like dogs. You could at least follow the example of Ivan Ivanovich and Ivan Nikiforovich. There you have friends who stay friends! What chums! What worthy men!" – That's chums for you! Tell me, what's it about? Why?'

'It's a delicate matter, Demyan Demyanovich! It can't be told orally. Better to have the application read out. Here, take it from this side, it's more decent here.'

'Read, Taras Tikhonovich!' said the judge, addressing the secretary.

Taras Tikhonovich took the application and, after blowing his nose the way that all secretaries in district courts do, with the aid of two fingers, he began to read:

'From nobleman of the district of Mirgorod and landowner Ivan, son of Ivan, Pererepenko a petition; to which refer the following points:

1) Known to the whole world for his impious and lawbreaking actions, which inspire loathing and exceed all bounds, nobleman Ivan, son of Nikifor, Dovgochkhun on the seventh day of July of this year 1810 occasioned me mortal offence, both personally in relation to my honour and equally in the debasement and confusion of my rank and family name. The aforesaid nobleman, himself moreover of vile appearance, is of quarrelsome character and filled with all kinds of blasphemy and abusive words!'

At this point the reader paused for a moment in order to blow his nose once more, while the judge folded his arms reverentially and merely said to himself, 'What a lively pen! Lord God! How this man can write!'

Ivan Ivanovich asked him to read on, and Taras Tikhonovich continued:

'The aforesaid nobleman Ivan, son of Nikifor, Dovgo-chkhun, when I came to him with amicable propositions, called me publicly by an offensive name, defamatory to my honour, viz. *a goose*, whereas it is known to the entire district of Mirgorod that I have by no means ever been called after this vile creature and have no intention of being so called in the future. Whereas the proof of my noble origin lies in the fact that in the register of births held in the church of The Three Prelates is recorded both the date of my birth and equally the christening received by me. Whereas *goose*, as is known to all in any way cognisant with learning, cannot be recorded in the register of births, since a *goose* is not a man, but a fowl, which fact is reliably known to all, even those not having attended the seminary. But the aforesaid malignant nobleman, being cognisant with all this, for no other reason than to cause mortal offence to my rank and title called me by the aforesaid vile name.

2) This very same improper and indecent nobleman moreover made an attempt upon my genealogy, received by me after my parent, being of the clerical calling, Ivan, son of Onisy, Pererepenko of blessed memory, in that contrary to all laws he transferred to a point directly opposite my porch a goose coop, which was done with no other intention than to aggravate the offence caused me; since the aforesaid coop stood heretofore in a tolerable site and was still quite sound. But the repulsive intention of the aforementioned nobleman consisted solely in causing me to be witness to improper events; for it is well-known that no man will enter a coop, the more so a goose coop, on decent business. In the course of this

unlawful deed, the two foremost supporting posts seized my own land, passed on to me within his own lifetime by my parent, Ivan, son of Onisy, Pererepenko of blessed memory, starting from the barn and in a straight line to the very spot where the peasant women wash their pots.

3) The aforedepicted nobleman, whose very forename and family name inspire all kinds of revulsion, nurtures in his heart the malicious intent to set light to me in my own home. The indubitable signs of which are evident from the following: firstly, the aforesaid malignant nobleman has begun to emerge frequently from his rooms, which previously, owing to his idleness and vile corpulence of body, he never undertook; secondly, in his servants' quarters, abutting the very fence enclosing the land received by me from my late parent of blessed memory, Ivan, son of Onisy, Pererepenko, a light burns daily and for an unusual length of time, which is in itself clear evidence, since before this, owing to his miserly meanness, not just the tallow candle, but even the night-light was always extinguished.

And for this reason I request the aforesaid nobleman Ivan, son of Nikifor, Dovgochkhun, being guilty of arson, of insulting my rank, name and family name, and of predatory acquisition of property, and above all of the prejudicial addition to my family name of the name *goose*, to be sentenced to the exaction of a fine and the settlement of expenses and losses, and the same, being the transgressor, to be put in chains and, fettered, to be accompanied to the town gaol, and the resolution to this my petition to be carried out immediately and rigorously.

Written and composed by the nobleman and landowner of Mirgorod Ivan, son of Ivan, Pererepenko.'

Upon completion of the reading of the application, the judge went up to Ivan Ivanovich, took him by the button and began speaking to him something like this: 'What is it you're doing, Ivan Ivanovich? For the fear of God, give up this application, let it go! (May it go to the Devil!) Better take Ivan Nikiforovich by the hands, and kiss one another, and buy some Santorin or local wine from Nikopol, or just simply make some punch, and invite me along! We'll have a good drink together and forget about everything!'

'No, Demyan Demyanovich! It's not that sort of matter,' said Ivan Ivanovich, with the air of importance that always suited him so well. 'It's not the sort of matter that can be resolved with an amicable agreement. Farewell! Farewell to you too, gentlemen!' he continued with the same air of importance, addressing everyone. 'I hope that my application will have the appropriate effect,' and he departed, leaving the entire courtroom in a state of astonishment.

The judge just sat there without a word. The secretary took snuff, the clerks overturned the base of the broken bottle that they used instead of an ink-well, and the judge himself absentmindedly spread the puddle of ink around the table with his finger.

'What do you say to that, Dorofey Trofimovich?' said the judge, turning to the clerk of the court after a period of silence.

'I don't say anything,' replied the clerk of the court.

'The things that go on!' continued the judge. He hadn't finished saying this before the door let out a crack and the front half of Ivan Nikiforovich landed in the courtroom. The arrival of Ivan Nikiforovich, in court what's more, seemed so extraordinary that the judge shrieked and the secretary broke off from his reading. One of the clerks, wearing a frieze imitation of a half-tailcoat, took his pen between his lips; the other swallowed a fly. Even the invalided soldier who performed the duties of courier and guard, and who until then had been standing by the door, scratching underneath his dirty shirt with a stripe on the shoulder, even this invalid gawped and trod on somebody's foot.

'To what do we owe the pleasure? What news? How's your health, Ivan Nikiforovich?'

But Ivan Nikiforovich was petrified, for he was jammed in the doorway and could not take a step either forwards or backwards. In vain did the judge call into the ante-room at the front for someone out there to give Ivan Nikiforovich a shove into the courtroom from the rear. In the ante-room there was only one old woman petitioner who, in spite of all the efforts of her bony arms, could do nothing. Then one of the clerks, with thick lips and broad shoulders, a fat nose, eyes that gazed drunk and disorderly, and ragged elbows, approached the front half of Ivan Nikiforovich, crossed his arms for him like a child and winked at the aged invalid, who stuck his knee into Ivan Nikiforovich's belly; and, despite his piteous groans, the latter was squeezed out into the ante-room. Then the bolts were shot back and the other half of the double doors opened. And the clerk and his assistant, the invalid, breathing hard through their mouths after their concerted efforts, diffused such a strong smell, that for a while the courtroom was all but turned into a public house.

'You're not hurt, are you, Ivan Nikiforovich? I'll tell my mother, and she'll send you an infusion, which you'll just have to rub on your waist and back and it'll all be better.'

But Ivan Nikiforovich collapsed into a chair and, other than lengthy ohs, he could say nothing. Finally, in a weak voice scarcely audible from exhaustion, he pronounced, 'Would you like?' and, taking the horn from his pocket, added, 'Help yourself!'

'I'm very glad to see you,' answered the judge. 'But I still can't imagine what made you take the trouble and favour us with such a pleasant surprise.'

'An application...' was all that Ivan Nikiforovich could utter.

'An application? What application?'

'A writ...' At this point his shortage of breath occasioned a lengthy pause: 'Oh!... With a writ on that villain... Ivan Ivanov Pererepenko.'

'Good Lord! You too! Such rare friends! A writ on such a virtuous man!...'

'He is Satan himself!' pronounced Ivan Nikiforovich abruptly.

The judge crossed himself.

'Take the application, read it.'

'There's nothing for it; read it, Taras Tikhonovich,' said the judge, turning to the secretary with an air of displeasure, moreover his nose involuntarily sniffed at his upper lip, which until then it had usually done only in great pleasure. Such arbitrariness on the part of his nose caused the judge still more annoyance. He took out his handkerchief and brushed all the snuff from his upper lip to punish its impertinence.

The secretary, after the normal overture that he always employed before the commencement of reading, that is, without the aid of a handkerchief, began in his normal voice thus:

'The application of the nobleman of the district of Mirgorod Ivan, son of Nikifor, Dovgochkhun, to which refer the following points:

39

1) In his hateful malice and evident animosity, the self-styled nobleman Ivan, son of Ivan, Pererepenko, initiates sundry dirty tricks, losses and other spiteful and horrifying actions against me, and yesterday afternoon, like a robber and thief, with axes, saws, chisels and other carpentry tools, made his way by night into my yard and into my very own coop, situated therein. With his own hands and in an abusive manner he chopped it up. For which I on my part had given no cause to such an unlawful and brigandly action.

2) The aforesaid nobleman Pererepenko has designs on my very life and until the seventh day of last month, keeping this intention secret, came to me and began in a friendly and cunning way to ask me for the gun which was to be found in my room, and offered me in exchange for it, with his characteristic miserliness, many useless items, such as: a brown pig and two sacks of oats. But foreseeing then his criminal intent, I tried in all manners to disincline him from the aforesaid, but the aforesaid villain and scoundrel Ivan, son of Ivan, Pererepenko cursed me in peasantly fashion and has nurtured towards me from that time irreconcilable enmity. Moreover the aforesaid, oft-mentioned savage nobleman and brigand Ivan, son of Ivan, Pererepenko is also of highly defamatory origins: his sister was a slut known to the whole world and went off after the company of chasseurs stationed in Mirgorod five years ago; while she registered her husband as a peasant. His father and mother were also most lawless people and were both unimaginable drunkards. The nobleman and robber already referred to, Pererepenko, by his bestial and reprehensible actions

has exceeded his whole family and under the guise of piety commits the most seductive deeds. Fasts he does not keep; for on the eve of the Christmas fast this apostate purchased a ram and on the next day ordered his unlawful girl, Gapka, to slaughter it, with the excuse that he ostensibly needed fat at that very moment for night-lights and candles.

For this reason I request that the aforesaid nobleman, being a brigand, sacrilegious villain, already detected in robbery and thieving, be fettered in chains and accompanied to prison or state gaol, and there, as is seen fit, being deprived of ranks and nobility, be soundly thrashed with barberry twigs and imprisoned in a penal colony in Siberia as required, that he be ordered to reimburse expenses and losses, and that the resolution be carried out according to this my petition. To this petition set his hand the nobleman of the district of Mirgorod Ivan, son of Nikifor, Dovgochkhun.'

As soon as the secretary finished the reading, Ivan Nikiforovich took hold of his hat and bowed with the intention of leaving.

'Where are you going, Ivan Nikiforovich?' said the judge in his wake. 'Have a seat for a little while! Drink some tea! Oryshko! Why are you standing there exchanging winks with the clerks, you stupid girl, off you go and bring some tea!'

But Ivan Nikiforovich, frightened at having ventured so far from home and undergone such a dangerous quarantine, had already managed to slip through the door, saying, 'Don't trouble, my pleasure...' and closed it behind him, leaving the entire courtroom in amazement.

There was nothing for it. Both applications were accepted, and the matter was preparing to take on an interest of some import, when one unforeseen circumstance made it even more absorbing. When the judge had left the courtroom in the company of the clerk of the court and the secretary, and the clerks were packing into a sack the chickens, eggs, chunks of bread, pies, buns, and other rubbish brought along by petitioners, it was then that a brown pig ran into the room and seized, to the astonishment of those present, not a pie or a crust of bread, but Ivan Nikiforovich's petition, which lay on the end of the table with its pages hanging down over the edge. Seizing the paper, the brown sow ran off so quickly that not one of the court officials could catch it, despite the throwing of rulers and inkstands.

This extraordinary occurrence caused a dreadful fuss, because not even a copy had yet been made of it. The judge, i.e. his secretary and the clerk of the court, had a long discussion about such an unheard-of circumstance; finally a resolution was made to write a memorandum about it to the mayor, since the investigation of this matter was more the business of the civil police. Memorandum number 389 was sent to him that same day, and as a result of this there took place the rather curious interview about which readers can learn from the following chapter.

CHAPTER FIVE

*In which is related the conference between two persons
of esteem in Mirgorod*

No sooner had Ivan Ivanovich dealt with things in the household and gone out as usual to lie on the veranda, than to his
untold amazement he saw something red at his gate. It was the
mayor's red cuff, which received a polishing in equal measure
to his collar and was turning into patent leather along the
edges. Ivan Ivanovich thought to himself: 'It's no bad thing
that Pyotr Fyodorovich has come for a talk,' but was very
surprised to see that the mayor was walking extremely fast and
waving his arms about, which was usually highly rare for him.

Eight buttons were set on the mayor's uniform jacket, while
the ninth, ever since it had come off during the procession for
the consecration of the church two years before, had still not
been found by the policemen, even though the mayor always
asks during the daily reports made to him by the sergeants
whether the button has been found. These eight buttons of
his were set in the same way as peasant women plant beans:
one to the right, the next to the left. His left leg had been shot
through in his last campaign, and for that reason he limped a
little and threw it out so far to the side, that in so doing he
ruined almost all the work of the right leg. The quicker the
mayor worked with his foot-soldiers, the less they moved
forward. And for that reason, before the mayor had reached
the veranda, Ivan Ivanovich had had the time to become quite
bemused as to why the mayor was waving his arms about
so rapidly. It interested him all the more that the matter
seemed of extraordinary importance, for the mayor even had a
new sword with him. 'Hello, Pyotr Fyodorovich!' cried Ivan

Ivanovich, who, as has already been said, was very curious, and was quite unable to contain his impatience at the sight of the mayor taking the porch by storm, yet still not raising his eyes, and quarrelling with his foot-soldiers, who found it quite impossible to climb the step at the first time of asking.

'I bid good day to my dear friend and benefactor Ivan Ivanovich!' replied the mayor.

'Please be so good as to take a seat. You're tired, I can see, as your wounded leg is troubling…'

'My leg!' cried the mayor, throwing at Ivan Ivanovich one of those glances that a giant throws at a pygmy, or a pedantic scholar at a dancing-master. At this he stretched out his leg and stamped it on the floor. This bravery cost him dear, however, because his whole body rocked and his nose pecked at the handrail; but the wise guardian of order, disguising what had happened, recovered himself and put a hand into his pocket as if to get out his snuffbox.

'Concerning myself I can report to all, dearest friend and benefactor Ivan Ivanovich, that in my time I've made more difficult marches than that. Yes, I have, seriously. During the campaign of 1807 for example… Ah, I'll tell you how I climbed over a fence to visit a pretty German girl.' At this the mayor narrowed his eyes and gave a devilishly roguish smile.

'And where have you been today?' asked Ivan Ivanovich, wishing to interrupt the mayor and quickly turn him to the reason for his visit; he would have very much liked to ask what the mayor meant to announce; but his sophisticated knowledge of society presented him with all the rudeness of such a question, and Ivan Ivanovich had to get a grip on himself and wait for the answer, although his heart was pounding unusually hard.

'Allow me to tell you where I've been,' replied the mayor.

'Firstly I should report to you that the weather today is excellent…'

At these last words Ivan Ivanovich almost died.

'But if you'll allow me,' continued the mayor, 'I came to see you today on a most important matter.' At this point the mayor's face and bearing assumed that same anxious look with which he had stormed the porch. Ivan Ivanovich came back to life and trembled as if in a fever, taking no time, as was his wont, to ask the question: 'Important in what way? Is it really important?'

'Be so good as to understand: first and foremost may I be so bold as to report to you, dear friend and benefactor Ivan Ivanovich, that you… for my part, be so good as to understand, it's nothing to me, but the views of government, the views of government demand it: you have violated the order of decorum!'

'What is it you're saying, Pyotr Fyodorovich? I don't understand a thing.'

'For pity's sake, Ivan Ivanovich! How is it you don't understand a thing? Your very own beast stole a most important official document, and you can still say afterwards that you don't understand a thing!'

'What beast?'

'With permission, your very own brown pig.'

'And how am I to blame? Why does the court guard open the doors?'

'But Ivan Ivanovich, it's your own animal, so you must be to blame.'

'My humble thanks to you for comparing me with a pig.'

'Now I never said that, Ivan Ivanovich! I swear to God, I never said that! Be so good as to reason yourself in good conscience; you are without any doubt aware, that according to the views of the authorities, unclean animals are forbidden to stroll around the town, all the more so around the main streets of the town... You must yourself agree that this is a forbidden matter.'

'God knows what it is you're saying. It's a matter of great import that a pig got out into the street!'

'Allow me to report to you, allow me, do allow me, Ivan Ivanovich, it's quite impossible. What's to be done? The authorities demand – and we must obey. I can't deny that chickens and geese sometimes run into the street and even into the square, take note: chickens and geese; but even last year I issued a proclamation that pigs and goats shouldn't be allowed into public squares. And that proclamation I then ordered to be read out loud at a meeting before all the people.'

'No, Pyotr Fyodorovich, I can see nothing here other than your trying in every way you can to offend me.'

'Now that is something you cannot say, my dearest friend and benefactor, that I am trying to offend. You must remember yourself: I didn't say a word to you last year when you built your roof a good two feet higher than the prescribed measure. On the contrary, I pretended that I hadn't noticed it at all. Believe me, my dearest friend, even now I would have, so to speak... but my duty, in a word, obligation, demands that I look after cleanliness. Judge for yourself, when suddenly on the main street...'

'As if your main streets are so nice! All the peasant women go along there to throw out what they don't need.'

'Allow me to report to you, Ivan Ivanovich, that you are yourself offending me! That can sometimes happen, it's true, but for the most part only by the fence, sheds or storerooms, but that a sow in farrow should brazen its way onto the main street, into the square, that's such a business...'

'What's the matter, Pyotr Fyodorovich? After all, a pig is God's creation!'

'Agreed. The whole world knows that you're a learned man, you're familiar with the sciences and various other subjects. Of course, I never studied any sciences at all: I only started studying joined-up writing when I was almost thirty. After all, as you know, I rose from the ranks.'

'Hm!' said Ivan Ivanovich.

'Yes,' continued the mayor. 'In 1801 I was a lieutenant in 4th Company, the 42nd Regiment of Chasseurs. Our company commander, you might be so good as to know, was Captain Yeremeyev.' At this juncture the mayor dipped his fingers into the snuffbox which Ivan Ivanovich was holding open, and gave the snuff a good rub.

Ivan Ivanovich replied: 'Hm.'

'But it's my duty,' continued the mayor, 'to submit to the demands of the government. Do you know, Ivan Ivanovich, that the theft of an official document from court by anybody is subject, just like any other crime, to the criminal court?'

'I know well enough to teach you something, if you want. You could say that sort of thing about people – if you stole a document, for example; but a pig is an animal, God's creature!'

'That's all true, but the law says: guilty of theft – I beg you to listen carefully: guilty! There's no reference here to either family name, or gender, or title, so presumably even an animal can be guilty. Say what you like, but before the pronouncement of sentence to punishment the animal must be presented to the police as the violator of order.'

'No, Pyotr Fyodorovich!' retorted Ivan Ivanovich coolly. 'That won't happen!'

'As you wish, only I must follow the orders of the authorities.'

'Why are you trying to frighten me? You probably mean to send the one-armed soldier to fetch it. I'll order the serving-woman to see him off with a poker. He'll get his one remaining arm broken.'

'I don't dare argue with you. In that case, if you don't want to present it to the police, then make use of it as you wish. Stick it for Christmas whenever you like, and make gammon joints out of it, or eat it as it is. Only if you're going to make sausages, I would ask you to send me a couple of the ones that your Gapka is such an expert at making out of pig's blood and fat. My Agrafena Trofimovna is very fond of them.'

'I'll send you a couple of sausages with pleasure.'

'I shall be very grateful, dear friend and benefactor. Now allow me to say one more word to you: I have a commission both from the judge, and equally from all our acquaintances, so to speak, to reconcile you with your friend Ivan Niki-forovich.'

'What? With an ignoramus? That I should be reconciled with that boor! Never! It won't happen, it won't!' Ivan Ivanovich was in an extremely decisive state.

'As you wish,' replied the mayor, treating both nostrils to snuff. 'I don't dare give advice myself; however, allow me to report: here you are now squabbling, yet when you make it up…'

But Ivan Ivanovich began talking about catching quail, which was usually the case when he wanted to change the subject.

And so, having had no success at all, the mayor was obliged to set out for home.

CHAPTER SIX

*From which the reader can easily learn all
that is contained therein*

No matter how they tried in court to conceal the affair, on the
very next day the whole of Mirgorod had found out that Ivan
Ivanovich's pig had run off with Ivan Nikiforovich's application. The first to forget himself and let it slip was none other
than the mayor. When Ivan Nikiforovich was told about it, he
said nothing, only asking whether it was the brown one.

But Agafya Fedoseyevna, who was there at the time, again
began pestering Ivan Nikiforovich. 'Come on, Ivan Nikiforovich, people will laugh at you as though you were an idiot
if you put up with this! What sort of nobleman will you be
after this? You'll be worse than the peasant woman who sells
those honey cakes you like so much.'

And her tirelessness persuaded him! From somewhere she
got hold of a little middle-aged man, swarthy, and with
blotches all over his face, in a dark-blue frock-coat with
patches on the elbows, an out-and-out bureaucratic ink-well!
He rubbed tar on his boots, carried three pens behind each
ear, and in lieu of an ink-well had a glass phial tied to a button
by a lace; he could eat nine pies in one sitting and put a tenth
in his pocket, and could fit so much legal jargon on a sheet of
stamped paper that nobody was able to read it all in one go
without interruptions for coughing and sneezing. This little
imitation of a man dug around, worked himself into a sweat
writing, and finally concocted the following document:

'To the Mirgorod district court from nobleman Ivan, son of Nikifor, Dovgochkhun.

In consequence of my aforesaid petition, which being from me, nobleman Ivan, son of Nikifor, Dovgochkhun, referred to that jointly with the nobleman Ivan, son of Ivan, Pererepenko; to which the Mirgorod district court itself expressed its indulgence. And the aforesaid most insolent arbitrary behaviour of the brown pig, being maintained in secret and already having reached the ears of neutral parties. Insofar as the aforesaid admission and indulgence, being of criminal intent, is strictly liable to judgement; for the aforesaid pig being an ignorant animal, and the more so capable of the theft of the document. From which it is clearly evident, that the oft-mentioned pig could not have been otherwise than schooled to that end by the adversary himself, the self-styled nobleman Ivan, son of Ivan, Pererepenko, already detected in brigandage, attempted murder and sacrilege. But the aforesaid Mirgorod court, with its characteristic partiality, expressed an agreement secret to its person; without such agreement the aforesaid pig could in no manner have been permitted the theft of the document; for the Mirgorod district court is most well-equipped with personnel, whereof it is already sufficient to name a certain soldier, present in the waiting-room at all times, who, albeit with only one eye and a somewhat injured arm, has for the purpose of expelling a pig and striking it with a truncheon the most commensurate capacities. From which can be reliably seen the indulgence of the aforesaid Mirgorod court and incontrovertible division of the usurious profit arising therefrom in coincident reciprocity. And the aforesaid aforementioned brigand

and nobleman Ivan, son of Ivan, Pererepenko, having been exposed, was in collaboration. Wherefore I, Ivan, son of Nikifor, Dovgochkhun, bring to the requisite omniscience the aforesaid district court, that if from the aforesaid brown pig or the nobleman acting in concord with it, Pererepenko, the cited application is not exacted, and a decision on it not given justly and in my favour: then I, nobleman Ivan, son of Nikifor, Dovgochkhun, shall make a complaint about such unlawful indulgence of the aforesaid court to the Palace of Justice with the requisite formal transfer of the case – Nobleman of the district of Mirgorod, Ivan, son of Nikifor, Dovgochkhun.'

This application had its effect: the judge was a man, as all kind people usually are, of a cowardly disposition. He turned to the secretary. But the secretary emitted a thick 'hm' through his lips, and showed on his face that indifferent and devilishly ambiguous expression adopted by Satan alone, when he sees at his feet a victim running towards him. One course remained: to reconcile the two friends. But how was this to be approached when all attempts so far had been unsuccessful? However, it was resolved to try again; but Ivan Ivanovich announced bluntly that he would have none of it, and even got very angry. Ivan Nikiforovich, instead of replying, turned his back and didn't say a word. Then the case progressed with the extraordinary speed for which the courts of law are so famous. The document was dated, registered, numbered, sewn in and signed for, all in one and the same day, then the file was put in a cupboard, where it lay, and lay, and lay, for a year, a second year, a third; many a bride had time to get married, a new street was opened in Mirgorod, the judge had one molar and two eye-teeth drop out, more kids than before ran around Ivan

Ivanovich's yard; where they sprang from, God alone knows! As a reproach to Ivan Ivanovich, Ivan Nikiforovich built a new goose coop, albeit a little further back than the earlier one, and completely blocked himself off from Ivan Ivanovich, so that these worthy men hardly ever saw one another face to face – and the file continued to lie in the best possible order in the cupboard, which became marbled with ink stains.

Meanwhile, an event that was extremely important for the whole of Mirgorod took place.

The mayor gave a reception! Where am I to find the brushes and palette to depict the variety of the gathering and the magnificent feast? Take a clock, open it up, and look at what's going on inside! A dreadful muddle, isn't it? And now imagine that almost as many wheels, if not more, were standing in the middle of the mayor's yard. What britzkas and carriages were not to be found there? One was wide at the rear and narrow at the front; another was narrow at the rear and wide at the front. One was both a britzka and carriage at the same time; another was neither britzka, nor carriage; one looked like a huge haycock or a fat merchant's wife; another like a dishevelled Jew or a skeleton, not yet entirely free of skin; one in profile was a perfect long-stemmed pipe; another looked like nothing at all, representing some strange being, utterly formless and extremely fantastical. From the midst of this chaos of wheels and coach-boxes there towered the likeness of a carriage with a window taken from a room, crossed with a thick transom.

Coachmen in grey jackets, greatcoats and overcoats, in sheepskin hats and caps of all sizes, with pipes in their hands, led unharnessed horses around the yard. What a reception the mayor gave! Allow me to enumerate all who were there: Taras Tarasovich, Yevpl Akinfovich, Yevtikhy Yevtikhyevich, Ivan

Ivanovich, not that Ivan Ivanovich, but the other one, Savva Gavrilovich, our Ivan Ivanovich, Yelevfery Yelevferyevich, Makar Nazaryevich, Foma Grigoryevich... I can go no further! I haven't the strength! My hand is tired from writing! And how many ladies were there! Dusky and white-faced, tall and short, fat, like Ivan Nikiforovich, and some so slim that it seemed each of them could be hidden inside the scabbard of the mayor's sword. How many bonnets! How many dresses! Red, yellow, coffee-coloured, green, blue, new, turned, reshaped, shawls, ribbons, ridicules! Farewell, my poor eyes! You will be no use for anything after this spectacle. And what a long table was stretched out! And when all began to talk – what a noise they made! How could a mill, with all its millstones, wheels, cog-wheels and mortars, compete with that! I can't tell you for sure what they talked about, but one would imagine that it was about many pleasant and useful things, such as the weather, dogs, wheat, bonnets, stallions. Finally Ivan Ivanovich, not that Ivan Ivanovich, but the other one, who has only one eye, said, 'I find it very strange that my right eye,' (one-eyed Ivan Ivanovich always spoke of himself ironically), 'can't see Ivan Nikiforovich, Mr Dovgochkhun.'

'He didn't want to come!' said the mayor.

'How's that?'

'It's already two years, praise be to God, since they fell out with one another, Ivan Ivanovich and Ivan Nikiforovich that is, and where the one is, the other won't go, not for anything!'

'I can hardly believe it!' With this, one-eyed Ivan Ivanovich raised his eyes upwards and clasped his hands together. 'What now, if people with good eyes no longer live in peace, where then am I with my blind eye going to live in harmony!' Everybody started laughing their heads off at this. All were very fond of one-eyed Ivan Ivanovich, because the jokes he made were absolutely in the taste of the day; even the tall lean man in the flannelette frock-coat with the plaster on his nose, who until then had been sitting in the corner and had not once altered the expression on his face, even when a fly flew up his nose, this same gentleman rose from his seat and moved closer to the crowd standing around one-eyed Ivan Ivanovich. 'Listen!' said one-eyed Ivan Ivanovich, when he saw that he was surrounded by a respectable group. 'Listen, instead of staring at my blind eye, as you are now, instead of that, let's reconcile our two friends! Now Ivan Ivanovich is talking to the women and the girls, we'll quietly send for Ivan Nikiforovich and push them together.'

All were unanimous in accepting Ivan Ivanovich's proposal and determined to send home immediately to Ivan Nikiforovich to ask him to come to the mayor's for dinner at all costs. But the important question of who should be entrusted with this important mission plunged everyone into confusion. There was a long argument as to who was most able and skilled in the diplomatic sphere; finally it was unanimously decided to entrust all this to Anton Prokofyevich Golopuz. But first the reader needs to be acquainted somewhat with this remarkable character. Anton Prokofyevich was an utterly virtuous man in the full meaning of this word: if any of the esteemed people of Mirgorod give him a neck scarf or underpants, he thanks them; if somebody gives his nose a little tweak, even then he thanks them. If he was asked, 'Why is it, Anton Prokofyevich, that your frock-coat is brown, but the sleeves are blue?', he would generally always reply, 'You haven't even got one like that! Wait a little, once it's worn in, it'll all be the same!'

And so it is: the blue cloth began to turn to brown from the effect of the sun and is now perfectly suited to the colour of the frock-coat; but what is strange is that Anton Prokofyevich is in the habit of wearing his cloth coat in the summer, and nankeen in the winter. Anton Prokofyevich doesn't have a house of his own. He did have one at the end of town once, but he sold it, and with the money he got he bought a team of three bay horses and a small britzka, which he rode around in to stay with various landowners. But since they involved a lot of trouble and, what's more, money was needed to buy oats, Anton Prokofyevich exchanged them for a violin and a serving-wench, with a twenty-five-rouble note thrown in. Then Anton Prokofyevich sold the violin and exchanged the girl for a morocco leather and gold tobacco-pouch. Even now he has a tobacco-pouch like no one else. In return for this delight he can no longer ride from one village to another, but has to remain in town and spend the nights in various houses, especially those of the noblemen who took pleasure in tweaking his nose. Anton Prokofyevich likes to eat well, plays a fair game of snap and old maid; he was always in his element when doing as he was told, and so, taking his hat and stick, he immediately went on his way. But as he walked, he began to consider how he was to move Ivan Nikiforovich to come to the reception. The somewhat difficult character of this otherwise worthy man made his enterprise almost impossible. And how, indeed, is he to resolve to come, when getting up from his bed alone has cost him great effort? But supposing he gets up, how is he to go to the place where, as he doubtless knows, his irreconcilable enemy is to be found?

The more Anton Prokofyevich thought about it, the more obstacles he discovered. The day was close; the sun burned down; sweat poured off him in torrents. Despite the fact that people tweaked his nose, Anton Prokofyevich was quite a cunning man in many matters. He just wasn't very lucky in exchanges; he knew very well when you need to play the fool, and was sometimes able to make something of circumstances and instances where a clever man is rarely in a condition to avoid trouble. While his inventive mind was thinking up a way to persuade Ivan Nikiforovich, and he was already going boldly ahead to face anything, one unexpected circumstance somewhat perturbed him.

It does no harm at this point to inform the reader that Anton Prokofyevich had, among others, one pair of trousers with the strange feature that whenever he put them on, dogs always bit him on the calves. As ill luck would have it, on this day he had put on precisely those trousers. And therefore, no sooner had he devoted himself to his thoughts, than a terrible barking struck his hearing from all sides. Anton Prokofyevich's shouts were so loud, for nobody could shout louder than he, that not only did the peasant woman familiar to us and the inhabitant of the immeasurable frock-coat run out to meet him, but even the little boys from Ivan Ivanovich's yard scattered out towards him, and although the dogs only managed to bite one of his legs, still this greatly diminished his courage, and it was with a certain degree of timidity that he approached the porch.

CHAPTER SEVEN

And the last

'Ah, hello! What are you teasing the dogs for?' said Ivan Nikiforovich when he saw Anton Prokofyevich, because nobody spoke to Anton Prokofyevich other than in jest.

'May they drop dead, the lot of them! Who's teasing them?' replied Anton Prokofyevich.

'You're lying.'

'I swear to God, I'm not! Pyotr Fyodorovich has invited you to dinner.'

'Hm.'

'I swear to God! His invitation was so persuasive, it can't be expressed. How is it, he says, that Ivan Nikiforovich avoids me as if I were an enemy. He never drops in for a talk or a sit down.'

Ivan Nikiforovich stroked his chin.

'If, he says, Ivan Nikiforovich won't come now either, I don't know what to think: he must harbour some malicious intent towards me! Be so kind, Anton Prokofyevich, as to persuade Ivan Nikiforovich! Well then, Ivan Nikiforovich, shall we go? There's excellent company gathered there at the moment!'

Ivan Nikiforovich began examining the cockerel which was standing on the porch and screeching with all its might.

'If only you knew, Ivan Nikiforovich,' continued the eager deputy, 'what sturgeon and fresh caviar Pyotr Fyodorovich has been sent!'

At this Ivan Nikiforovich turned his head and began listening carefully.

This encouraged the deputy. 'Let's go, quickly; Foma

Grigoryevich is there too! What's the matter with you?' he added, seeing that Ivan Nikiforovich was still lying in the same position. 'Well then? Are we going or not?'

'Don't want to.'

This 'don't want to' amazed Anton Prokofyevich. He'd already been thinking that his persuasive presentation had completely won over this man, a worthy man, after all, but instead of that he had heard a decisive 'don't want to'.

'And why don't you want to?' he asked, almost with the annoyance that he displayed extremely rarely, even when people put burning paper on his head, something the judge and mayor particularly enjoyed doing for amusement.

Ivan Nikiforovich took some snuff.

'As you please, Ivan Nikiforovich, but I don't know what's holding you back.'

'What should I go for?' Ivan Nikiforovich finally pronounced. 'The brigand will be there!' That was what he usually called Ivan Ivanovich. Good God! And was it so long ago...

'I swear to God, he won't! As God is holy, he won't! May I be struck down on this very spot!' replied Anton Prokofyevich, who was prepared to swear ten times an hour. 'Let's go now, Ivan Nikiforovich!'

'But you're lying, Anton Prokofyevich, he's there, isn't he?'

'I swear it, I swear to God, he isn't! May I be rooted to the spot if he's there! And simply judge for yourself, why should I be lying? May my arms and legs wither and drop off! What, do you still not believe me? May I drop dead right here before you! May the Heavenly Kingdom never be seen by my father, my mother or me! You still don't believe me?'

Ivan Nikiforovich was completely reassured by these protestations and ordered the valet in the boundless frock-coat to bring his baggy trousers and nankeen coat with the pleated skirt.

I assume that a description of Ivan Nikiforovich putting on his trousers, having his tie wound around his neck and finally putting on his coat, which split under the left sleeve, is quite superfluous. Let it suffice that during all this time he maintained a decent composure, and replied not one word to Anton Prokofyevich's propositions to exchange something for his Turkish tobacco-pouch.

Meanwhile, the gathering was awaiting impatiently the decisive moment when Ivan Nikiforovich would appear, and the universal desire for these worthy men to become reconciled with one another would finally be fulfilled; many were almost certain that Ivan Nikiforovich wouldn't come. The mayor even wanted to have a bet with one-eyed Ivan Ivanovich that he wouldn't come, backing down only because one-eyed Ivan Ivanovich demanded that he put up his wounded leg against his own blind eye, at which the mayor took great offence, while the company had a quiet laugh. Nobody had yet sat down at the table, although it was well past one o'clock, a time at which in Mirgorod, even on special occasions, dinner should have long been under way.

No sooner had Anton Prokofyevich appeared in the doorway, than, at that same moment, he was surrounded by everyone. In answer to all the questions, Anton Prokofyevich shouted a single decisive word: he won't; no sooner had he pronounced this, and as a storm of reprimands, scoldings and perhaps tweaks as well was preparing to fall on his head for the failure of his embassy, than the door suddenly opened, and in walked Ivan Nikiforovich.

If Satan himself or a ghost had appeared, they would not have produced such amazement as that into which the whole group was thrown by the unexpected arrival of Ivan Niki-forovich. And Anton Prokofyevich clutched his sides and simply roared with joy at having played such a trick on the entire company.

Whatever the case, it was still all but incredible to everyone that Ivan Nikiforovich could have dressed as befits a nobleman in such a short time. Ivan Ivanovich wasn't present at this point; he had left the room for some reason. Recovering from its amazement, the entire company took an interest in Ivan Nikiforovich's health and expressed its pleasure that he had expanded in girth. Ivan Nikiforovich exchanged kisses with all and sundry, saying, 'Most obliged'. Meanwhile the smell of borsch carried through the room and tickled pleasantly at the nostrils of the famished guests. Everyone piled into the dining-room. A line of ladies, garrulous and taciturn, skinny and fat, stretched on ahead, and the long table became speckled with every colour. I shan't begin to describe the dishes there were at table! I'll make no reference to the cottage-cheese patties in sour cream, nor to the giblets served with the borsch, nor to the turkey with plums and raisins, nor to the dish which looked very much like boots soaked in kvass, nor to that sauce which is the swansong of the ancient cook, the sauce served completely engulfed in flaming wine, which was very amusing and at the same time frightening for the ladies. I shan't begin to mention these dishes, because I much prefer eating them to talking about them at length. Ivan Ivanovich really liked the fish cooked with horseradish. He became particularly busy with the useful and nourishing exercise of eating it. Picking out the finest fish bones, he was putting them on the plates when somehow by chance he glanced up across the table: Heavenly Creator, how strange it was! Opposite him sat Ivan Nikiforovich. At that very same moment Ivan Nikiforovich glanced up too!… No, I can't do it! Give me another pen! My pen is limp, dead, has too fine a nib for this picture! Their faces, reflecting their amazement, seemed to turn to stone. Each of them saw a face long familiar, which he might have been thought ready to approach spontaneously, as an unexpected friend, offering his horn with the words, 'help yourself' or 'dare I beg you to do me the favour?'; yet equally, the same face was terrifying, like a bad omen! Sweat poured in torrents from both Ivan Ivanovich and Ivan Nikiforovich. Those present, all of them, however many there were at the table, were struck dumb in their attention and couldn't tear their eyes from the former friends. The ladies, who until then had been busy with a rather interesting conversation about how capons are produced, suddenly cut the conversation short. All fell quiet! It was a picture worthy of the brush of a great artist! Finally Ivan Ivanovich pulled out his handkerchief and began blowing his nose; while Ivan Nikiforovich looked around and settled his gaze on the wide-open door. The mayor noticed this movement immediately and ordered the door to be tightly shut. Then both of the friends began eating, and thereafter they did not once glance at each other.

As soon as dinner was over, both of the erstwhile friends leaped from their seats and began searching for their hats so as to slip away. Then the mayor gave a wink, and Ivan Ivanovich, not that Ivan Ivanovich, but the other one with the blind eye, stood behind Ivan Nikiforovich's back, while the mayor went round the back of Ivan Ivanovich, and they both began pushing them from the rear so as to shove them together and not release them until they had offered their hands. Ivan Ivanovich with the blind eye pushed Ivan Nikiforovich perhaps a little crookedly, but still quite successfully, and towards the spot where Ivan Ivanovich was standing; but the mayor steered a course too far to the side, because he simply could not manage his self-willed infantry, which on this occasion would not obey any command at all, and as if on purpose kicked out an extremely long way and in completely the opposite direction (which possibly happened because there had been an extremely large number of various liqueurs at the table), so that Ivan Ivanovich fell over onto a lady in a red dress, who, out of curiosity, had thrust her way through to the very middle. Such an omen augured nothing good. However, to put things right, the judge took the place of the mayor and, drawing all the snuff from his upper lip with his nose, he shoved Ivan Ivanovich back in the other direction. This is the customary method of reconciliation in Mirgorod. It rather resembles a ball game. As soon as the judge had shoved Ivan Ivanovich, Ivan Ivanovich with the blind eye, leaning with all his might against his man, shoved Ivan Nikiforovich, from whom the sweat was streaming like rainwater from a roof. Despite the fact that both the friends dug their heels in, still they were pushed together, because both of the active parties received significant reinforcement from the other guests.

Then they were closely surrounded on all sides, not to be released until they resolved to offer one another their hands. 'God be with you, Ivan Nikiforovich and Ivan Ivanovich! Admit, in all conscience, what it is you've fallen out over: isn't it mere trifles? Don't you feel ashamed before men and before God?'

'I don't know,' said Ivan Nikiforovich, panting in exhaustion (it was noticeable that he was not at all averse to a reconciliation), 'I don't know what it was I did to Ivan Ivanovich; why did he chop down my coop and lay plans to destroy me?'

'I'm innocent of any malicious intent,' said Ivan Ivanovich, keeping his eyes turned away from Ivan Nikiforovich. 'I swear before God and before you, honoured noblemen, I've done nothing to my enemy. Why is it he abuses me and does damage to my rank and title?'

'What damage have I done to you, Ivan Ivanovich?' said Ivan Nikiforovich. Another minute of discussion and the old enmity was set to be extinguished. Ivan Nikiforovich's hand was already in his pocket to get out his horn and say, 'Help yourself'.

'Is it not damage, then,' replied Ivan Ivanovich, without raising his eyes, 'when you, my good sir, have insulted my rank and name with a word that cannot decently be mentioned here?'

'Permit me to say this as a friend, Ivan Ivanovich!' (With this Ivan Nikiforovich touched Ivan Ivanovich's button with his finger, which signified how complete his good disposition was.) 'You took offence at the Devil knows what; at the fact that I called you a *goose*...' Ivan Nikiforovich suddenly realised that he had been incautious in uttering this word; but it was already too late: the word had been uttered.

Everything went to the Devil!

When at the utterance of this word without witnesses Ivan Ivanovich had lost his temper and flown into such a rage, the like of which may God grant one never to see a man in – what now, then, judge for yourselves, kind readers, what now, when this deadly word was uttered at a gathering where there was a host of ladies, before whom Ivan Ivanovich liked to be especially seemly? Had Ivan Nikiforovich acted differently, had he said fowl rather than goose, things could still have been put right.

But everything was at an end!

He threw one glance at Ivan Nikiforovich – and what a glance! If that glance had been given executive power, then it would have turned Ivan Nikiforovich to dust. The guests understood this glance and themselves hastened to separate them. And this man, the model of meekness, who never omitted to question a single beggar-woman, ran out in a terrible fury. Such are the mighty storms aroused by passions!

For a whole month nothing was heard of Ivan Ivanovich. He locked himself in his house. The cherished chest was unlocked, and from the chest was brought out – what? Silver roubles! Old silver roubles of his grandfather's time! And these silver roubles passed into the ink-stained hands of money-grubbing pen-pushers. The case was transferred to the Palace of Justice. And when Ivan Ivanovich received the joyous announcement that it would be resolved tomorrow, only then did he look out at the world and resolve to leave the house. Alas! From that time on the Palace announced that the case would be concluded tomorrow every day over the course of ten years!

About five years ago I was passing through the town of Mirgorod. I was travelling at a bad time. It was autumn then, with its sad, damp weather, mud and mist. Some sort of unnatural greenery, the work of miserable, continual rains, covered the pastures and cornfields like a liquid net, and it stuck to them like mischief to an old man and roses to an old woman. The weather had a powerful influence on me at that time: when it was miserable, I was miserable. But in spite of this, as I began to approach Mirgorod I felt that my heart was beating hard. God, how many memories! I had not seen Mirgorod for twelve years. There lived here then in touching friendship two unique men, two unique friends. But how many renowned men had died off! The judge, Demyan Demyanovich, was then already deceased; Ivan Ivanovich with the blind eye had departed this life as well. I drove into the main street: everywhere there stood poles with wisps of straw attached to the tops: some new street layout was being effected! Several huts had been demolished. The remains of their fences and wattle hurdles stuck up dejectedly.

That day was a holy day; I ordered my bast-covered wagon to be halted by the church and I entered so quietly that nobody noticed. To tell the truth, there was nobody there to notice. The church was empty. Hardly any people. It was evident that even the most devout were put off by the mud. The candles on this overcast, or to put it better, sickly day were somehow strangely unpleasant; the elongated windows with their round panes of glass were flooded with tears of rain. I went back to the porch and turned to a venerable, grey-haired old man. 'Permit me to enquire whether Ivan Niki-forovich is alive?' At this moment the lamp before an icon flared up more brightly and the light struck directly onto the face of the man beside me. How surprised I was, when on examination I saw familiar features! It was Ivan Nikiforovich himself! But how he had changed! 'Are you well, Ivan Niki-forovich? How you've aged!' – 'Yes, I've aged. I've been to Poltava today,' replied Ivan Nikiforovich.

'What's that you say? You've been to Poltava in such bad weather?' – 'What can one do? The lawsuit...' At this I let out an involuntary sigh. Ivan Nikiforovich noticed this sigh and said, 'Don't worry, I'm reliably informed that the case will be resolved next week, and in my favour.' I shrugged my shoulders and went to try and learn something about Ivan Ivanovich.

'Ivan Ivanovich is here!' someone told me. 'He's in the choir.' Then I noticed a skinny figure. Can that be Ivan Ivanovich? The face was covered in wrinkles, the hair was completely white; but the coat was still the same. After the initial greetings, Ivan Ivanovich, addressing me with the cheerful smile that always suited his funnel-shaped face so well, said, 'Should I notify you of a pleasant piece of news?' – 'What news is that?' I asked. 'My case is to be resolved tomorrow without fail. The Palace said it's certain.'

I gave an even deeper sigh, hurried to say goodbye quickly, because I was travelling on a very important matter, and got into my wagon. The scrawny nags, known in Mirgorod as courier horses, began moving forward, their hooves producing a noise unpleasant to the ear as they sank into the grey mass of the mud. The rain poured down onto the Jew who sat on the coach-box, sheltering under some bast matting. The damp cut right through me. The sad town gate with its sentry box, in which an invalid was repairing his grey armour, moved slowly by. The same fields once more, dug up in places, black, turning green in places, wet jackdaws and crows, the monotonous rain, the tearful sky without a ray of hopeful light. – This is a miserable world, gentlemen!

Olde-Worlde Landowners

I am very fond of the modest life of those secluded owners of isolated villages who are generally called olde-worlde in Little Russia, and who are like decrepit, picturesque cottages, attractive in their motley appearance and complete contrast to some nice, smooth new building whose walls have not yet been washed by the rain, whose roof has not been covered in green mould, and whose porch has not been stripped of its plaster to reveal its red bricks. I sometimes like to descend for a short time into the realm of this unusually secluded life where not a single wish flies beyond the picket fence surrounding the little yard, beyond the wattle hurdles of the orchard, filled with apple and plum trees, beyond the huts of the village that surround it, slumping over on their sides, shaded by willow, elder and pear trees.

The life of their modest owners is so quiet, so quiet, that for a moment you forget yourself and imagine that passions, desires and those troublesome fruits of the evil spirit that disturb the world do not exist at all, and you have only seen them in a brilliant, glittering dream. I can see from here the low cottage with its gallery of small, blackened wooden pillars going all around the house, so that during thunder and hail one can close the shutters on the windows without getting soaked by the rain. Beyond it is fragrant bird cherry, whole rows of squat fruit trees, drowning in the crimson of cherries and the amber sea of plums, coated with a matt, leaden bloom; the branching maple, in whose shade a rug is spread out for relaxation; in front of the house the spacious yard, with its fresh, low-growing grass and a trampled path from barn to kitchen, and from kitchen to master's rooms; a long-necked goose drinking water with its baby goslings, delicate as down; the picket fence, hung with bunches of dried pears and apples and rugs put out to air, the cartload of melons standing beside the barn, the unharnessed ox lying idly beside it – all this holds an inexpressible charm for me, perhaps because I see it all no longer, and everything from which we are parted is dear to us.

Be that as it may, still even then, whenever my britzka approached the porch of this cottage, my spirit would assume an astonishingly pleasant and peaceful state; the horses trotted cheerfully up to the porch, the coachman climbed down in leisurely fashion from the coach-box, and filled his pipe as if he were arriving at his very own house; even the barking that arose from the phlegmatic Rovers, Rexes and Fidos was pleasurable to my ears. But best of all I liked the owners of these modest little corners themselves, the little old men and women who emerged solicitously to meet you. Even now their faces sometimes appear to me in the noise and the crowd amidst fashionable tailcoats, and then a state of somnolence suddenly comes upon me and visions of the past arise. Always written on their faces is such kindness, such cordiality and sincerity, that you unwittingly reject, for a short time at least, all your audacious dreams, and all your sensibilities imperceptibly shift towards a humble bucolic life.

To this day I am unable to forget two old people of the last century who, alas, are no longer with us, but my soul is to this day still filled with pity and my sensibilities are strangely contracted when I imagine how with time I shall once again visit their former, now deserted abode and see a pile of tumbledown huts, a choked pond, an overgrown ditch on the spot where their low cottage stood – and nothing more. Sad! In advance I feel sad! But let us turn to our story.

Afanasy Ivanovich Tovstogub and his wife, Pulcheria Ivanovna Tovstogubess, to use the expression of the local peasants, were those old people of whom I began to tell. If I were a painter and wanted to depict Philemon and Baucis[1] on canvas, I would never choose any other model than them.

Afanasy Ivanovich was sixty, Pulcheria Ivanovna fifty-five. Afanasy Ivanovich was tall, and always went about in a ram-fleece coat covered with camlet, sat hunched up, and was almost always smiling, even if relating something or simply listening. Pulcheria Ivanovna was rather serious and almost never laughed; but in her face and eyes was written so much kindness, so much readiness to entertain you with all the very best she had, that you would doubtless have found a smile just too sickly sweet on her kind face. The light wrinkles on their faces were disposed so pleasantly that an artist would prob-ably have stolen them. It seemed that one could read in them the whole of their lives, the clear, peaceful lives led by the old, native, simple-hearted, yet rich families which are always the antithesis of those base Little Russians who fight their way up from the ranks of tar-mixers or petty tradesmen and fill the palaces of justice and government departments like locusts, who steal the last kopek from their fellow-countrymen, flood St Petersburg with complainants, finally make some capital and triumphantly add to their surnames, which end with the letter *o*, the letter *v*. No, they were not like those contemptible and pitiful creatures, no more than any other ancient and native Little Russian families. It was impossible to look at their mutual love without sympathy. They always addressed each other formally, using forename and patronymic: Afanasy Ivanovich; Pulcheria Ivanovna. 'Was it you that broke the chair, Afanasy Ivanovich?' – 'Never mind, don't be cross, Pulcheria Ivanovna: it was I.' They never had children, and as a result all their affection was concentrated on themselves. Once, in his youth, Afanasy Ivanovich served in the volunteer regiments and was later a second major, but that was already a very long time ago, it was already in the past, and Afanasy Ivanovich himself hardly ever reminisced about it now.

Afanasy Ivanovich married when he was thirty, when he was a fine young fellow and wore an embroidered waistcoat; he even carried Pulcheria Ivanovna off quite adroitly when her relatives did not want her to marry him; but of that too he now remembered very little, or at least he never spoke about it. All these distant, unusual events had been transformed long ago or replaced by a peaceful and secluded life, those somnolent and also somehow harmonious reveries that you experience while sitting on a rural balcony that faces the garden, with the beautiful rain making its glorious noise as it slaps onto the leaves of the trees and runs off in babbling streams, casting a spell of drowsiness over your limbs, while in the meantime the rainbow steals out from behind the trees and shines its seven matt colours across the sky in the form of a crumbling vault. Or when your carriage rocks you as it dives between the green bushes, while the steppe quail's cry rings out and the fragrant grass, the ears of corn and the wild flowers all climb into the carriage doors, striking you lightly on the hands and face.

He always listened with a pleasant smile to the guests that visited him, sometimes even talked himself, but mostly asked questions. He was not one of those old men who bore you with their eternal praise for the old days or censure of the new. On the contrary, when asking you questions, he displayed great curiosity and concern for the circumstances of your own life, the successes and failures that all kind old people are generally interested in, although it is rather like the curiosity of the child who, while talking with you, is examining the engraving on your watch. Then his face could be said to breathe kindness.

The rooms of the cottage in which our old people lived

were small and low-ceilinged, as normally encountered in the homes of olde-worlde people. Each room had a huge stove occupying almost one third of it. These little rooms were awfully warm, because both Afanasy Ivanovich and Pulcheria Ivanovna were very fond of warmth. The stove doors all opened out into the entrance hall, which was always filled almost to the very ceiling with the straw that is generally used in Little Russia instead of firewood. The crackling of this burning straw and the lighting make the entrance hall extremely pleasant on a winter's evening when you run into it, clapping your hands together, frozen stiff after your pursuit of some brunette or other. The walls of the rooms were decorated with several pictures, large and small, in ancient narrow frames. I am certain that the master and mistress had themselves forgotten their content long ago, and if some of them had been taken away, they would probably not have noticed. Two portraits were large and painted in oils. One represented some bishop, the other the Emperor Peter III. From out of a narrow frame gazed the Duchess La Vallière, all soiled with flies. Around the windows and above the doors there was a host of those small pictures which you somehow grow accustomed to taking for stains on the wall, and so you do not look at them at all. The floor was of clay in almost all the rooms, but it was so neatly laid out, and was maintained with a degree of tidiness probably not used to maintain a single parquet floor in a wealthy household, lazily swept by a sleepy gentleman in livery.

Pulcheria Ivanovna's room was completely full of trunks, chests, boxes and caskets. A myriad bundles and bags of seeds from flowers, vegetables and watermelons hung on the walls. A myriad balls of multi-coloured wool, scraps of material from ancient dresses that had been made half a century before were packed away in the corners in chests and between chests. Pulcheria Ivanovna was a great housewife and collected everything, although sometimes she did not know herself what it would all be used for later. But the most remarkable things in the house were the singing doors. As soon as morning was approaching, the singing of doors rang out through the whole house. I cannot say why they sang; whether it was the rusted hinges that were to blame, or whether the very workman who made them had hidden some secret inside them; but the remarkable thing is that every door had its own particular voice; the door leading into the bedroom sang in the thinnest descant; the door that led into the dining-room was a hoarse bass; but the one that was in the entrance hall emitted some strange tinkling and at the same time moaning sound, so that, if you listened to it closely, you could finally clearly hear: 'mercy me, so cold!' I know that many people do not like this sound at all, but I am very fond of it, and if I sometimes happen to hear the creaking of doors here, then I suddenly get a real whiff of the countryside, a little low-ceilinged room lit by a candle in an ancient candlestick, dinner already standing on the table, the dark May night looking in from the garden through the wide-open window at the table with its places set, a nightingale pouring its trills over the garden, the house and the distant river, the fear and rustling of the branches... and God, what a long line of memories am I plunged into then! The chairs in the room are the wooden, bulky ones that the old days are generally known for; they all had high, chiselled backs in their natural state without any varnish or paint; they were not even covered with any fabric and were rather similar to the chairs that bishops sit on to this very day. Triangular side-tables in the corners, rectangular ones in front of the sofa and the mirror in its slender gold frame with chiselled leaves, which the flies have bespattered with black spots, in front of the sofa a carpet with birds that look like flowers and flowers that look like birds – there you have almost all the decoration of the undemanding cottage where my old people lived.

The maids' room was bursting with young and not-so-young girls in striped petticoats who were sometimes given little bits of sewing to do by Pulcheria Ivanovna, and who were made to prepare berries for cooking, but who for the most part ran back and forth to the kitchen and slept. Pulcheria Ivanovna considered it essential to keep them in the house, and kept a strict watch on their morals. Yet to her extreme surprise, no more than a few months would pass without the waist of one or other of her girls becoming much fuller than normal; this seemed all the more surprising since there were almost no bachelors in the house, except perhaps for just the serving-boy who went about in a grey half-tailcoat and bare feet and who, if not eating, was certain to be asleep. Pulcheria Ivanovna would generally scold the culprit and punish her severely so that it would not happen again. On the window-panes there hummed a dreadfully large number of flies which were all drowned out by the rounded bass of a bumble-bee, sometimes accompanied by the piercing shrieking of wasps; but as soon as the candles were lit, this entire gang set off for its nightly lodgings and covered the whole of the ceiling in a black cloud.

Afanasy Ivanovich did very little about the estate, although, incidentally, he did sometimes ride out to see the mowers and reapers and watched their work quite intently; the whole burden of management lay on Pulcheria Ivanovna. Pulcheria Ivanovna's housekeeping consisted in the constant unlocking and locking of the storeroom, in pickling, drying and boiling an innumerable host of fruits and plants. Her house was utterly reminiscent of a chemical laboratory. Under an apple tree there was a fire eternally laid out; and a cauldron or copper bowl of jam, jelly or comfiture made with honey, with sugar or I do not remember what else, was hardly ever removed from the iron tripod.

Under another tree the coachman was eternally distilling in a copper alembic vodka flavoured with peach leaves, bird-cherry flowers, centaury, cherry stones, and by the end of this process he was in no state whatsoever to control his tongue: he would talk such nonsense that Pulcheria Ivanovna could not understand a thing, and he would go off to the kitchen for a sleep. Such quantities of all this rubbish were boiled up, pickled and dried, that they would doubtless have flooded the entire yard in the end, because Pulcheria Ivanovna, in addition to what was calculated to be for use, always liked to prepare some more to have in reserve, if the better half of it had not been eaten up by the yard-girls, who, getting into the store-room, gorged themselves there so dreadfully that they spent the whole day groaning and complaining of their stomachs.

Pulcheria Ivanovna had little opportunity to go into the tillage and other aspects of the farming. The steward, joining forces with the village elder, robbed them in merciless fashion. They established the custom of going into the landowners' woods as though they were their own, made a great quantity of wooden sledges and sold them at the nearest market; apart from that they sold all the thick oak trees to the local Cossacks to be felled to build mills. Only once did Pulcheria Ivanovna wish to inspect her woodland. To this end the droshky was harnessed up with its enormous leather aprons, because of which, no sooner had the coachman shaken the reins, and the horses, which had once served in the militia, set off, than the air was filled with strange sounds, so that suddenly there could be heard both a flute, and tambourines, and a drum; every nail and iron fastening rang to such an extent that they could hear right over by the mills that the mistress was driving out of the yard, although the distance was not less than a mile and a quarter. Pulcheria Ivanovna could not help but notice the terrible devastation in the wood and the loss of the oak trees which even as a child she had known as centenarians.

'Why is it, Nichipor,' she said, turning to the steward who was also there, 'that you've let the oaks get thinned out so? See your hair doesn't get thin.'

'Why have they thinned out?' the steward said in a matter-of-fact way. 'They've died! Yes, died off completely: struck by lightning, gnawed away by the worms – they've died, mistress, died.'

Pulcheria Ivanovna was quite satisfied with this reply and, returning home, gave the order only to double the guard in the orchard by the Spanish cherry trees and the big snow pears. Those worthy managers, the steward and the village elder, found it quite superfluous to bring all the flour into the master's barns, for half would be quite enough for him; in the end, even this half was brought in mouldy or damp, after being rejected at the market. But no matter how much the steward and the village elder stole, no matter how dreadfully everyone in the yard stuffed themselves, from the housekeeper to the pigs, who annihilated an awfully large quantity of plums and apples and often pushed a tree with their own snouts to shake down from it a whole shower of fruits, no matter how much the sparrows and crows pecked, how much the whole yard took presents to their gossips in other villages and even pinched the old linen and yarn from the barns, all of which returned to the source of all life, i.e. to the tavern, no matter how much was stolen by guests, phlegmatic coachmen and menservants, still the blessed earth produced everything in such quantities, and Afanasy Ivanovich and Pulcheria Ivanovna needed so little, that all this dreadful thieving seemed quite insignificant in their domestic economy.

Both the old people, following the ancient custom of olde-worlde landowners, were very fond of eating. As soon as dawn began to break (they always rose early) and the doors started up their dissonant concert, they were already at the table drinking coffee. After drinking his fill of coffee, Afanasy Ivanovich went out into the entrance hall and, shaking his handkerchief, said, 'Shoo, shoo! Get off the porch, you geese!' He generally came across the steward in the yard. As a rule, he entered into conversation with him, questioned him about his jobs in the greatest detail, and passed on such comments and orders as would have surprised anybody with their unusual knowledge of husbandry, and any novice would not have dared even to think of being able to steal from such a vigilant master. But his steward was a wise old bird: he knew how he should reply, and still better how he should run things.

After this, Afanasy Ivanovich returned to the living quarters and, going up to Pulcheria Ivanovna, said, 'Well then, Pulcheria Ivanovna, perhaps it's time we had a bite of something to eat?'

'What could we have to eat now, then, Afanasy Ivanovich? Maybe flat cakes with pork fat, or poppy-seed pies, or perhaps pickled mushrooms?'

'All right, some mushrooms, if you please, or some pies,' replied Afanasy Ivanovich, and on the table there suddenly appeared a tablecloth with pies and mushrooms.

An hour before lunch Afanasy Ivanovich had something to eat again, drank vodka from the old silver goblet, accompanying it with mushrooms, various dried fish and so on.

They sat down to lunch at twelve o'clock. Besides the dishes and sauce-boats, there stood on the table a host of little pots with sealed lids so that no appetising item of traditional, tasty cuisine could lose its smell or flavour. Over lunch the conversation was generally about subjects most closely related to the meal.

'This porridge seems a little burnt to me,' Afanasy Ivanovich would usually say. 'Does it seem that way to you, Pulcheria Ivanovna?'

'No, Afanasy Ivanovich. Put a little more butter on, then it won't seem burnt, or else take this mushroom sauce and pour some of that on it.'

'As you wish,' said Afanasy Ivanovich, holding out his plate. 'Let's see how it is.'

After lunch Afanasy Ivanovich went for an hour's rest, after which Pulcheria Ivanovna brought him a sliced watermelon and said, 'Here, Afanasy Ivanovich, try this nice watermelon.'

'Don't put your trust, Pulcheria Ivanovna, in the fact that it's red in the middle,' said Afanasy Ivanovich, taking a respectable slice. 'It can sometimes be red, yet not nice.'

But the watermelon quickly disappeared. After this Afanasy Ivanovich also ate up several pears and set off for a walk in the garden together with Pulcheria Ivanovna. Returning home, Pulcheria Ivanovna went off about her business, while he sat down on the porch facing the yard and watched the storeroom continually revealing and concealing its interior, and the girls pushing each other as they took in or brought out piles of rubbish of all sorts in wooden crates, sieves, trays and other fruit containers. A little later he would send for Pulcheria Ivanovna, or go to find her himself, and say, 'What could I have to eat, Pulcheria Ivanovna?'

'What could you have?' Pulcheria Ivanovna would say.

'Maybe I'll go and tell them to bring you some of the fruit dumplings that I specially ordered to be left for you?'

'That would be nice,' replied Afanasy Ivanovich.

'Or perhaps you might eat some blancmange?'

'That would be good,' replied Afanasy Ivanovich. After which all this was immediately served up and, as is the way, eaten.

Before supper Afanasy Ivanovich had a bite of something else. They sat down to supper at half past nine. Straight after supper they went off to sleep again, and universal silence reigned in this busy, yet still peaceful corner. The room where Afanasy Ivanovich and Pulcheria Ivanovna slept was so hot that rare would be the person capable of remaining in it for several hours. But in addition, to be warmer, Afanasy Ivanovich slept on the stove-bench, although the great heat often made him get up several times during the night to take a turn around the room. Sometimes, while walking about the room, Afanasy Ivanovich would groan.

Then Pulcheria Ivanovna would ask, 'Why are you groaning, Afanasy Ivanovich?'

'God knows, Pulcheria Ivanovna, my stomach seems to be aching a bit,' said Afanasy Ivanovich.

'Perhaps you might eat something, Afanasy Ivanovich?'

'I don't know whether that would be a good idea, Pulcheria Ivanovna! Still, what could I have to eat?'

'Some sour milk or some thin compote with dried pears.'

'If you please, maybe just a little to try,' said Afanasy Ivanovich. A sleepy serving-girl went to rummage through the cupboards, and Afanasy Ivanovich ate a plateful; after which he usually said, 'I seem to feel better now.'

Sometimes, if the weather was clear and the rooms were quite well heated, Afanasy Ivanovich became cheerful and liked to tease Pulcheria Ivanovna by talking about something inappropriate.

'So, Pulcheria Ivanovna,' he said, 'what if our house suddenly caught fire, where would we go?'

'God preserve us!' said Pulcheria Ivanovna, crossing herself.

'But just suppose that our house burnt down, where would we move to then?'

'God knows what you're talking about, Afanasy Ivanovich! How could it happen that our house should burn down: God wouldn't allow it.'

'But what if it did burn down?'

'Well then we'd move into the kitchen. For the time being you could have the little room that the housekeeper uses.'

'And what if the kitchen burnt down too?'

'May God preserve us from such a calamity, that both the house and the kitchen should burn down together! Well then it would be into the storeroom until a new house had been built.'

'And what if the storeroom burnt down too?'

'God knows what you're talking about! I don't even want to listen to you! It's a sin to say things like that, and God punishes such talk.'

Still Afanasy Ivanovich, pleased at having had a joke at Pulcheria Ivanovna's expense, sat smiling on his chair.

But the old people seemed to me most interesting of all when they had guests. Then everything in the house took on a new appearance. These kind people could have been said to live for their guests. All the very best they had, it was all brought out. They vied with one another in their attempts to entertain you with all that their household could produce. But most pleasant of all for me was the fact that in all their eagerness to oblige there was no excessive sweetness. Their cordiality and readiness to please were expressed so meekly in their faces and suited them so well that you acceded, like it or not, to their requests. These were the result of the pure, clear simplicity of their kind, guileless souls. This cordiality was not at all like that with which you are entertained by an official from the revenue department, who has made his way in the world courtesy of your efforts, who calls you his benefactor and grovels at your feet. There was no way that a guest would be allowed to leave on the same day: he would have to spend the night without fail.

'How can you set off on such a long journey at such a late hour!' Pulcheria Ivanovna always said (the guest usually lived two or three miles away from them).

'Of course,' said Afanasy Ivanovich. 'Anything might happen: you could be attacked by robbers or some other scoundrel.'

'May God spare us from robbers!' said Pulcheria Ivanovna. 'And why mention such things at bedtime. Robbers or no robbers, it's dark and not the time for travelling at all. Then there's your coachman, I know your coachman, he's so puny and small, any mare could knock him down. What's more, he's probably already got tipsy and gone to sleep somewhere.'

And the guest would have to stay without fail; however, the evening spent in a cosy, low-ceilinged room, the cordial, warming and soporific conversation, the spreading clouds of steam from the food served at the table, always nourishing and skilfully prepared, are his reward. I can see Afanasy Ivanovich now, sitting bent over on his chair with his permanent smile, listening to his guest with attention and even pleasure! Often the talk would be of politics. The guest, who also very rarely left his village, with an air of importance and a mysterious expression often voiced his conjectures, and told of how the French had made a secret pact with the English to let Bonaparte loose on Russia once more, or simply told of the imminent war, and then Afanasy Ivanovich often said, pretending not to look at Pulcheria Ivanovna, 'I'm thinking of going off to war myself; why shouldn't I go off to war?'

'Now he's away!' interrupted Pulcheria Ivanovna. 'Don't you believe him,' she said, turning to the guest. 'How's an old man like him to go off to war! The first soldier he meets will shoot him! I swear to God, he'll shoot him! Just like that, he'll take aim and shoot him!'

'Well,' said Afanasy Ivanovich, 'I'll shoot him too.'

'Just listen to him talk!' continued Pulcheria Ivanovna. 'How's he to go off to war! Even his pistols went rusty long ago and just lie around in the storeroom. If you could only see them: they're the sort that would be blown apart by the powder before he had the chance to fire them. And he'd injure his hands, disfigure his face and be wretched for the rest of his life.'

'Well,' said Afanasy Ivanovich, 'I'll buy myself some new armament. I'll take a sabre or a Cossack lance.'

'This is pure fantasy. He gets something into his head all of a sudden and starts his tales,' continued Pulcheria Ivanovna in annoyance. 'I know he's joking, but it's unpleasant listening to it all the same. He always comes out with such things that sometimes you listen, and listen, and then you take fright.'

But Afanasy Ivanovich, pleased at having frightened Pulcheria Ivanovna a little, sat and laughed, bent over on his chair.

Pulcheria Ivanovna was most interesting of all for me when she led a guest up to the hors d'oeuvres. 'This here,' she would say, removing the stopper from a carafe, 'is vodka infused with milfoil and sage. If someone has aching shoulder-blades or back, then this is a great help. This one here is flavoured with centaury: if there's a ringing in your ears or a rash across your face, it's a great help. And this one is distilled with peach stones – here, take a glass, what a lovely smell. If you somehow give yourself a knock on the corner of a cupboard or a table when getting out of bed, and a bump comes up on your forehead, you only have to drink one glass before supper, and it disappears as if by magic – it clears up that minute as if it had never been there at all.' After this there followed a similar listing of the other carafes, and they almost always had some sort of healing properties. After loading the guest with this entire medicine chest, she led him up to a host of plates standing ready. 'This here is mushrooms with germander! These are with cloves and walnuts; I was taught how to pickle them by a Turkish woman when we still had Turkish prisoners here. She was such a kind woman, and you didn't notice at all that she was of the Turkish faith. She behaved in almost exactly the same way as us; only she didn't eat pork: said that it was forbidden somewhere in their laws. This here is mushrooms with currant leaves and nutmeg! And this here is mullet; this is the first time I've pickled them; I don't know what they're like; I learned the secret from Father Ivan. First of all you have to spread oak leaves out in a small tub, then you sprinkle them with pepper and saltpetre, and on top of that you add the flower you can find on tarragon, so you take this flower and you spread the tails out vertically. And these here are pies! These are cheese pies, these are poppy-seed pies! And these are the ones that Afanasy Ivanovich is very fond of, made with cabbage and buckwheat.'

'Yes,' added Afanasy Ivanovich, 'I'm very fond of them: they're soft and just a little sour.'

In general Pulcheria Ivanovna was in extremely good spirits

whenever they had guests. The kind old woman! She devoted herself entirely to her guests. I liked visiting them, and although I overate dreadfully, like everyone else who stayed with them, and although it was not at all good for me, still I was always glad to go and see them. I wonder, incidentally, whether the very air in Little Russia does not have some special quality that aids digestion, because if anyone took it into his head to eat his fill like that here, there is no doubt that he would end up lying not in bed, but on the table.

The kind old people! But my narrative is approaching a most sad event which changed the life of this quiet corner for ever. This event will appear all the more striking, in that it had its origins in the most insignificant incident. But such is the strange way of things that it is always paltry causes that have given birth to great events and, on the other hand, great enterprises that have ended with insignificant consequences. Some conqueror or other gathers all the might of his state, wages war for several years, his generals become famous, and eventually it all ends with the acquisition of a plot of land with no space even to sow a few potatoes; whereas sometimes, on the other hand, two sausage-makers or other in two towns will start a fight between themselves over some nonsense, and the quarrel will eventually embrace the towns, then the hamlets and villages, and at last the whole state. But let us leave these deliberations; they have no place here. Moreover, I dislike deliberations when they remain only deliberations.

Pulcheria Ivanovna had a little grey cat which almost always lay curled up in a ball at her feet. Pulcheria Ivanovna sometimes stroked her and used a finger to tickle her neck, which the spoilt little cat stretched up as high as she could. It cannot be said that Pulcheria Ivanovna was too fond of her, but she had simply become attached to her, being accustomed to seeing her all the time. Afanasy Ivanovich, however, often mocked this attachment.

'I don't know, Pulcheria Ivanovna, what it is you see in the cat. What use is she? If you had a dog, that would be another matter: you can take a dog out hunting, but what use is a cat?'

'You be quiet, Afanasy Ivanovich,' said Pulcheria Ivanovna. 'You just like talking and nothing else. A dog is dirty, a dog will make a mess, a dog will break everything, but a cat is a quiet creature, she'll do no one any harm.'

Cats or dogs, it was all one to Afanasy Ivanovich anyway; he only spoke like that to tease Pulcheria Ivanovna a little.

Beyond the garden they had a big wood which had been completely spared by the enterprising steward, perhaps because the knocking of the axe would have reached the ears of Pulcheria Ivanovna herself. It was dense and neglected, old tree trunks were covered with thickly growing hazel and resembled the shaggy legs of doves. In this wood there lived wild tom-cats. Wild woodland cats should not be confused with those daredevils that run around the roofs of houses. Those that are found in towns, their stern temper notwithstanding, are much more civilised than the inhabitants of the woods. These are quite the opposite, for the most part an uneducated and wild race; they always go around skinny, their miaowing is coarse and unrefined. They sometimes dig their way through underground passages right into the barns and steal the pork fat, they can appear even in the kitchen itself by jumping in suddenly through the open window when they notice that the cook has gone for a walk in the long grass. In general, no noble feelings are familiar to them; they lead a predatory life and throttle little sparrows in their very own nests.

These tom-cats spent a long time with Pulcheria Ivanovna's

meek little cat as they sniffed at one another through the hole under the barn, and finally they enticed her to join them, the way a detachment of soldiers entices a foolish peasant girl. Pulcheria Ivanovna noticed the disappearance of the cat and sent people out to search for her, but the cat was nowhere to be found. Three days passed; Pulcheria Ivanovna felt sorry, but in the end completely forgot about her. One day, when she had been inspecting her kitchen garden and was returning with fresh green cucumbers, picked by her own hand for Afanasy Ivanovich, her ear was struck by the most piteous mewing. As if by instinct she called 'puss-puss,' and suddenly, from out of the long grass there emerged her grey cat, thin and skinny; it was evident that she had not had a bite to eat for several days now. Pulcheria Ivanovna carried on calling her, but the cat stood in front of her, mewing and not daring to come close; it was clear that she had grown very wild since the old days. Pulcheria Ivanovna went on ahead, continuing to call the cat, which followed her fearfully right up to the fence. Finally, when she saw formerly familiar parts, she even went into the house. Pulcheria Ivanovna ordered her to be given some milk and meat straight away and, sitting in front of her, took pleasure in the greed with which her poor favourite swallowed piece after piece of meat and gulped down the milk. The grey fugitive grew fatter almost before her eyes and no longer ate so greedily. She reached her hand out to stroke her, but the ingrate had clearly already become too accustomed to the predatory tom-cats, or else had picked up the romantic principle that poverty with love is better than a palace, and the tom-cats were as poor as church mice; whatever the case, she jumped out of the window, and none of the yard-servants was able to catch her.

The old woman fell deep into thought: 'That was my death

coming to fetch me!' she said to herself, and nothing could dispel the idea. She was miserable all day. In vain did Afanasy Ivanovich make jokes and try to find out why she had suddenly become so sad: Pulcheria Ivanovna was unresponsive, or else responded in a way that could not possibly satisfy Afanasy Ivanovich. On the next day she had grown noticeably thinner.

'What is the matter with you, Pulcheria Ivanovna? You're not ill, are you?'

'No, I'm not ill, Afanasy Ivanovich! I want to announce a special event to you: I know I am going to die this summer: my death has already been to fetch me!'

Afanasy Ivanovich's lips became somehow abnormally twisted. However, he tried to conquer the sad feeling in his soul, and with a smile he said, 'God knows what you're talking about, Pulcheria Ivanovna! Instead of that decoction you often take, you've probably been at the peach vodka.'

'No, Afanasy Ivanovich, I haven't had any peach vodka,' said Pulcheria Ivanovna.

And Afanasy Ivanovich regretted teasing Pulcheria Ivanovna like that, and he looked at her, a tear hanging on his eyelash.

'Afanasy Ivanovich, I beg you to carry out my will,' said Pulcheria Ivanovna. 'When I die, bury me alongside the church fence. Dress me in my grey dress, the one with the little flowers on a brown field. Don't dress me in the satin dress, the one with the crimson stripes: a dead woman doesn't need a dress any more. What use is it to her? But it'll come in useful for you: you can have a smart dressing-gown made from it for when guests come, so that you can look respectable to receive them.'

'God knows what you're talking about, Pulcheria Ivanovna!'

said Afanasy Ivanovich. 'Death will come someday, but now you're scaring me with these words of yours.'

'No, Afanasy Ivanovich, I already know when my death is to be. But don't you grieve over me: I'm already an old woman and I've lived long enough, and you're already old too, we'll meet soon enough in the other world.'

But Afanasy Ivanovich sobbed like a child.

'It's a sin to cry, Afanasy Ivanovich! Don't sin and anger God with your sorrow. I don't regret that I'm dying. I only regret one thing,' (a heavy sigh interrupted her speech for a moment). 'I regret the fact that I don't know who to leave you with, or who will look after you when I die. You're like a little child: you need to be loved by the one that will take care of you.' As she spoke, the expression on her face was one of such deep, such shattering, heartfelt pity, that I do not know if anybody could have looked upon her with equanimity at that moment.

'Look here, Yavdokha,' she said, turning to the housekeeper, who had been specially summoned on her orders, 'when I die, you're to look after the master, take care of him as you would your own eye, your own child. See that they cook what he likes in the kitchen, that you always give him clean linen and clothes; and when there are guests, see that you dress him up decently, otherwise he may well sometimes come out wearing his old dressing-gown, because even now he often forgets when it's a holy day and when it isn't. Don't take your eyes off him, Yavdokha, I'll be praying for you in the other world, and God will reward you. Don't you forget, Yavdokha, you're old already, you've not got long to live, don't burden your soul with sin. If you don't look after him, you'll have no happiness on earth. I shall myself ask God not to allow you a good end. And you yourself will be wretched, and your children will be wretched, and none of your family will have God's blessing in anything.'

The poor old woman! At that time she was thinking neither of the great moment that awaited her, nor of her own soul, nor of her future life; she was thinking only of her poor companion, with whom she had spent her life and whom she was leaving orphaned and homeless. With unusual dispatch she arranged everything in such a way that Afanasy Ivanovich would not notice her absence after she had gone. Her conviction of her imminent demise was so strong, and her spiritual state was so attuned to it, that a few days later she did indeed take to her bed and could no longer eat any food. Afanasy Ivanovich was transformed into the very soul of attentiveness and never left her bedside. 'Perhaps you might have something to eat, Pulcheria Ivanovna?' he said, looking into her eyes with disquiet. But Pulcheria Ivanovna did not speak. Finally, after a long silence, she moved her lips as if she wanted to say something – and she breathed her last.

Afanasy Ivanovich was utterly crushed. It seemed so outlandish to him, he did not even cry. He gazed at her with dull eyes, as if he did not realise the full significance of the corpse.

They laid the deceased out on a table, dressed her in that very dress that she had herself appointed, folded her arms in the sign of the cross, put a wax candle in her hand – he gazed at all this insensibly. A host of people of all kinds filled up the yard, a host of guests came for the funeral, long tables were set out in the yard, there were heaps of the traditional funeral *kasha*, sauces, pies, the guests talked, cried, gazed at the deceased, discussed her qualities, looked at him; but he himself gazed strangely at all this. The deceased was carried away at last, the people flocked behind, and he followed her; the priests were in their full vestments, the sun was shining, infants cried in their mothers' arms, skylarks sang, children in their shirt-tails ran and frisked along the way. Finally the coffin was set down above the grave, he was told to go up and kiss the deceased for the last time: he went up and kissed her, and tears appeared in his eyes, but they were somehow insensible tears. The coffin had been lowered, the priest had taken a spade and been the first to throw in a handful of earth, the deep, mournful choir of the reader and two sextons had sung to her eternal memory beneath a clear, cloudless sky, the workmen had taken up their spades, and earth had already covered and levelled out the grave – and at this point he made his way forward; everybody stepped aside and gave him room, wanting to know his intention. He raised his eyes, looked in confusion and said, 'So you've already gone and buried her! Why?!' He stopped, and did not finish his speech.

But when he returned home, when he saw that his room was empty, that even the chair on which Pulcheria Ivanovna used to sit had been removed – he sobbed, sobbed loudly, sobbed inconsolably, and the tears flowed like a river from his dim eyes.

Five years passed from that day. What grief is not borne away by time? What passion can survive the uneven battle with it? I knew a man at the height of his still youthful powers, full of true nobility and virtues, I knew him in love, tenderly, passionately, wildly, audaciously, modestly, and before me, almost before my eyes, the object of his passion – tender and beautiful as an angel – was struck down by insatiable death. I have never seen such terrible spasms of spiritual suffering, such wild, burning anguish, such consuming despair as those that rocked the unfortunate lover. I never thought a man could create such a hell for himself, in which there was not a shadow, not a shape, nothing that might in any way resemble hope…

People tried not to let him out of their sight; they hid from him every instrument with which he might destroy himself. After two weeks, all of a sudden he conquered himself: he began to laugh and joke; he was given his freedom, and the first thing he used it for was to buy a pistol. One day, a shot suddenly rang out and gave his family a terrible fright. They ran to his room and saw him lying outstretched with a shattered skull. The doctor who then appeared, and whose skill was the talk of the town, saw signs of life in him, found the wound to be not quite mortal, and, to the astonishment of all, he recovered. The watch on him was increased still further. Even at table they did not lay a knife beside him, and they tried to remove everything with which he might strike himself; but in a short time he found a new opportunity and threw himself under the wheels of a passing carriage. His arm and leg were smashed to pieces, but again he recovered. A year later I saw him in a crowded hall: he was sitting at a table, covering a card and cheerfully saying, '*Petit-ouvert*,' while behind him, leaning on the back of the chair and playing with his counters, there stood his young wife.

At the end of the said period of five years after the death of Pulcheria Ivanovna, while in those parts I dropped in to Afanasy Ivanovich's little farmstead to pay a call on my old neighbour, with whom I had once spent many a pleasant day and where I had always eaten my fill of the finest creations of the cordial hostess. As I approached the yard, the house seemed to me to have doubled in age, the peasants' huts had quite fallen onto their sides, in the same way as their owners doubtless had too. The picket fence and wattle hurdles in the yard were completely ruined, and I myself saw the cook pulling stakes out as kindling for the stove, when she only needed to take an extra two steps to reach the brushwood that was piled up in the same spot. It was with sadness that I drove up to the porch; those same Rovers and Rexes, blind now or with broken legs, began barking, lifting up their undulating tails, hung about with burdock. An old man came out to meet me. So it's him! I recognised him straight away; but he was now twice as bent as before. He recognised me and greeted me with the same smile that I had known. I followed him indoors; everything there seemed to be as before; but in everything I noticed a strange disorder, a sort of palpable absence of something; in a word, I felt within myself those strange emotions which overcome us when we enter for the first time the home of a widower we have previously known as inseparable from the helpmeet who has accompanied him all his life. These emotions are similar to those when we see before us the man we have always known as healthy with one leg missing. In everything could be seen the absence of the solicitous Pulcheria Ivanovna: at table one knife was laid that had no handle; the food was no longer prepared with the same skill. I did not want so much as to ask about the housekeeping, I was even afraid just to take a look at the working areas.

When we sat down at the table, a serving-girl tied on a napkin for Afanasy Ivanovich, and it was a good thing too, because otherwise he would have stained the whole of his dressing-gown with sauce. I tried to keep him interested and told him various pieces of news; he listened with the same smile, but at times his gaze was quite insensible, and the thoughts in it did not so much wander as disappear. He often picked up a spoonful of porridge and, instead of taking it to his mouth, he took it to his nose; instead of sticking his fork into a piece of chicken, he jabbed at the carafe with it, and then the serving-girl took his hand and aimed it at the chicken. We sometimes waited several minutes for the next course. Afanasy

Ivanovich noticed this himself and said, 'Why do they take so long bringing the food?' But I could see through the gap in the door that the boy bringing us the dishes was not thinking about that at all and was asleep, with his head resting on a bench.

'This is the dish,' said Afanasy Ivanovich when we were served curd-cheese patties with sour cream, 'this is the dish,' he continued, and I noticed that his voice had begun to tremble, and a tear was preparing to pop out of his leaden eyes, but he was making every effort in his desire to restrain it. 'This is the dish that the... the... the la... the late...' and suddenly the tears poured out. His hand fell onto the plate, the plate overturned, went flying and smashed, he was completely covered in sauce; he sat insensible, insensibly holding his spoon, and the tears flowed and flowed in torrents, like a stream, like an incessantly gushing fountain, onto the napkin that covered him.

God! I thought, looking at him: five years of all-conquering time – and the old man is already insensible, the old man whose life seemed never to have been troubled by a single powerful spiritual sensation, whose whole life seemed to have consisted only of sitting on a high chair, of eating dried fish and pears, of kind-hearted stories – and such a long-lasting, such a burning sorrow? Which then has the greater power over us: passion or habit? Or all powerful impulses, the entire whirlwind of our desires and boiling passions – are they only a consequence of our brilliant youth, and is it for that reason alone they seem deep and shattering? Be that as it may, at this moment all our passions seemed to me childish, set against this long, slow, almost insensible habit. He made several efforts to pronounce the dead woman's name, but in mid-word his quiet and ordinary face contorted convulsively, and the crying of a child struck me to the very heart. No, these were not the tears with which the old are normally so generous as they represent to you their pitiful state and misfortunes: nor were these the tears that they shed over a glass of punch; no! these were tears that flowed without permission, of their own accord, accumulating through the bitter pain of a heart that has already grown cold.

He did not live long after this. I recently heard about his death. Strange, however, is the fact that the circumstances of his demise bore a certain resemblance to the demise of Pulcheria Ivanovna. One day, Afanasy Ivanovich resolved to take a little stroll around the garden. As he was walking slowly along a path with his normal nonchalance, without a thought in his head, a strange thing happened to him. He suddenly heard somebody behind him pronounce in quite a clear voice: Afanasy Ivanovich! He turned around, but there was absolutely nobody there, he looked in every direction, peered into the bushes – nobody anywhere. It was a still day, and the sun was shining. He fell into thought for a moment; his face livened up somehow, and at last he uttered, 'It's Pulcheria Ivanovna calling me!' You have doubtless at one time or another happened to hear a voice calling you by your name, something the common people explain thus: a soul is pining for someone and is calling to him to come; after which death inevitably ensues. I confess, I have always found this mysterious call terrifying. I remember that I often heard it in my childhood: sometimes somebody behind me would suddenly pronounce my name distinctly. When this happened the day was generally most bright and sunny; not a single leaf on a tree stirred in the garden, the silence was deathly, even the grasshopper stopped at this moment, there was not a soul in the garden; but, I confess, had the wildest and stormiest night with all the hell of the elements come upon me alone in the middle of an impenetrable forest, I would not have been so frightened of it as I was of this terrible silence in the midst of a cloudless day. I would then usually flee the garden in the greatest fear and with bated breath, and would only calm down when I met somebody coming towards me, whose appearance banished this terrible emptiness from my heart.

He submitted completely to his soul's conviction that Pulcheria Ivanovna was calling him, he submitted with the will of an obedient child, he withered, spluttered, melted like a candle, and finally went out like one, when there is no longer anything left that might sustain its poor flame. 'Lay me alongside Pulcheria Ivanovna,' is all he said before his end.

His wish was carried out and he was buried beside the church, near the grave of Pulcheria Ivanovna. There were fewer guests at the funeral, but there were just as many common people and beggars. The master's cottage had already become quite empty. The enterprising steward and the village elder had carried off to their own huts all the remaining old objects and junk that the housekeeper had not been able to walk off with. There soon arrived, from where is unknown, some distant relation, the heir to the estate, who had previously served as a lieutenant, in which regiment I do not recall, and who was a dreadful reformer. He saw at once the very great disorder and negligence in the affairs of the household; he resolved to be sure to root out everything, to correct and bring order to everything. He bought six splendid English sickles, nailed a special number to each hut, and finally arranged things so well that six months later the estate was taken into guardianship. The wise guardianship (consisting of a former district assessor and some staff-captain in a faded tunic) used up in a short period of time all the chickens and eggs. The huts, which had been almost completely lying on the ground, collapsed altogether; the peasants turned to drunkenness, and for the most part went on the run. While the true owner himself, who, incidentally, lived quite happily with his guardians and drank punch with them, visited his village very rarely and did not stay there for long. To this day he travels around all the fairs in Little Russia; he makes thorough enquiries and weighs up the prices on various major wholesale products, such as flour, hemp, honey and so on, but he buys only trifling little things, such as flints, pipe-cleaners and, in general, anything that does not exceed a wholesale price of one rouble.

The Carriage

The little town of B— grew much jollier when the *** cavalry regiment came to be stationed there. Whereas otherwise it is dreadfully dull. When you're riding through it and you happen to glance at the squat daub cottages that look onto the street in an unbelievably sour way, then… what happens then inside your heart just can't be expressed, there's a feeling of such anguish, it's as though you've either just lost at cards, or you've said something stupid at an inappropriate moment – in a word, it's not nice. The clay on them has fallen off because of the rain, and the walls, instead of being white, have turned skewbald; the roofs are mostly covered with reeds, as is usually the case in our southern towns; the little orchards were chopped down long ago by order of the mayor to improve the place's appearance.

You won't come across a soul in the streets, maybe just a cockerel might walk across the roadway, which is soft as a cushion from the dust that lies on it to a depth of six inches and turns to mud at the least drop of rain, and then the streets of the little town of B— are filled with those plump animals that the local mayor calls Frenchmen. Poking their serious snouts out from their baths, they set up such a grunting that it only remains for anybody riding by to drive his horses on all the quicker. But then it's hard to come across anybody riding by in the little town of B—. Rarely, very rarely, some landowner or other, who has eleven serfs, clatters along the roadway in some half-britzka, half-cart, wearing a nankeen frock-coat, peeping out from heaps of flour sacks, and whipping on the bay mare who has a foal running after her.

The market square itself has a rather sad appearance: the tailor's house looks out extremely foolishly, not presenting its full façade, but just one corner; opposite it some stone building with two windows has been under construction for about fifteen years; further on, a fashionable plank-fenced yard stands all on its own, painted grey to match the colour of the mud – this was erected by the mayor as a model for other edifices when he was young and had not yet acquired the habit of sleeping immediately after lunch, nor of drinking some decoction flavoured with dry gooseberries at bedtime. Everywhere else it's almost all wattle fencing; in the middle of the square are the smallest of shops; in them you can always see a bunch of ring-shaped rolls, a peasant woman wearing a red headscarf, three stone of soap, several pounds of bitter almonds, pellets for shooting, jean material, and two merchants' salesmen playing quoits by the doors at all hours.

But as soon as the cavalry regiment came to be stationed in the little provincial town of B—, everything changed. The streets were filled with colour, livened up, in a word, took on a completely new look. The squat cottages often saw a graceful, stately officer passing by with a plume on his head, going to visit a comrade to talk about promotion, about the most splendid tobacco, and sometimes, on the quiet from the general, to play cards for the droshky, which could be called the regimental droshky, because, without leaving the regiment, it managed to do the rounds of everybody; today it would be the major riding in it, tomorrow it would appear in the lieutenant's stable, and in a week's time, lo and behold, it would again be the major's batman greasing it with pork fat. The wooden fencing between the houses was everywhere dotted with soldiers' caps hanging in the sunshine; a grey greatcoat was inevitably sticking out somewhere on a gate; in the alleyways you could come across soldiers with moustaches as wiry as boot-brushes. You could see these moustaches all over the place. If the townswomen gathered at the market with their ladles, there were probably moustaches peeping out from over their shoulders. At the ancient place of execution a moustached soldier was absolutely certain to be lathering the beard of some bumpkin, who, with eyes bulging upwards, just croaked every now and then. The officers livened up society, which until then had consisted only of the judge, who lived in the same house as some deacon's wife, and the mayor, a reasonable man, but one who slept resolutely all day long: from lunchtime until the evening, and from the evening until lunchtime. Society became still more numerous and engaging when the quarters of the brigade-general were transferred here. The landowners of the district, at whose existence nobody would have guessed up until then, began to visit the little provincial town more frequently, to meet with the gentlemen officers, and sometimes to have a little game of faro, by that time an extremely dim dream in heads overburdened with sowing crops, running errands for wives and hunting hares.

It's a great pity I can't recall the circumstances that prompted the brigade general to give a grand luncheon; the preparations made for it were immense: the clattering of cooks' knives in the general's kitchen could be heard even in the vicinity of the town gate. The whole market was requisitioned in its entirety for the lunch, so that the judge and the deacon's wife had only flat cakes made with buckwheat flour and blancmange to eat. The small yard at the general's quarters was completely full of droshkies and carriages. The company consisted only of men: the officers and a few of the landowners of the district.

The most remarkable of all the landowners was Pythagor Pythagorovich Chertokutsky, one of the chief aristocrats of the province of B—, who had made more noise than anyone else at the elections and had made his appearance there in a very smart conveyance. He had served previously in one of the cavalry regiments and had numbered among its significant and prominent officers. At least, he was prominent at the many balls and gatherings wherever their regiment roamed; anyway, you can ask the young women of Tambov and Simbirsk about that. It's highly likely that he would have made an advantageous name for himself in other provinces too, had he not resigned his commission owing to a certain incident, usually known as a messy business: whether it was he who in the old days gave someone a slap in the face, or he that was given it, I don't remember for sure, only the fact of the matter is that he was asked to resign. In so doing, however, he didn't lessen his authority one bit: he wore a tailcoat with a high waist in the style of a military tunic, spurs on his boots and a moustache beneath his nose, because without it the nobility might have thought that he had served in the infantry, to which he referred contemptuously sometimes as the 'infantery', and sometimes as the 'infantility'. He was to be found at all the crowded markets to which the Russian heartland, consisting of nurses, children, daughters and fat landowners, flocked to have fun in britzkas, *tarataikas*, tarantasses and other coaches, the likes of which have never been seen even in anybody's dreams. His nose could sniff out where a cavalry regiment was stationed, and he always came to see the gentlemen officers. He would leap down before them most gracefully from his light carriage or droshky and get to know them extremely quickly. At the last elections he gave the nobility a fine lunch at which he announced that if they would only elect him marshal, he would put the noblemen on the very best footing. In general he behaved like a proper gentleman, as they put it in the rural districts and provinces, he married quite a pretty little thing, and acquired along with her a dowry of two hundred serfs and several thousand in capital. The capital was immediately used up on a team of six really excellent horses, gilt locks for the doors, a tame monkey for the house, and a French butler. Meanwhile the two hundred serfs, together with two hundred of his own, were mortgaged in aid of some financial dealings. In a word, he was a proper landowner... a very tolerable landowner. Besides him there were several other landowners at the general's lunch too, but there's nothing to say about them. All the rest were military men of the same regiment plus two staff-officers: a colonel and a rather fat major. The general himself was burly and corpulent, but he was a good boss, as the officers commented. His speaking voice was a rather deep and impressive bass.

The lunch was exceptional: the sturgeon, beluga, sterlets, bustards, asparagus, quail, partridges, mushrooms all served as proof that the chef hadn't had a hot meal since the previous day, and four soldiers with knives in their hands had worked all night helping him with *fricassées* and *gelées*. An endless supply of bottles, tall ones of Lafitte, short-necked ones of Madeira, a beautiful summer's day, the windows wide open, dishes of ice on the table, the top buttons undone on the gentlemen officers, the crumpled shirt fronts on the pro-prietors of roomy tailcoats, conversation going to and fro, drowned by the general's voice and drenched by the cham-pagne – everything went with everything else. After lunch they all rose with a pleasant weight in their bellies and, lighting up long- and short-stemmed pipes, they went out with cups of coffee in their hands onto the porch.

The general, the colonel and even the major had their tunics completely undone so that you could see just a little of their noble braces, made of some silky material, but the gentlemen officers, maintaining due respect, kept theirs done up, except for the top three buttons.

'So now you can take a look at her,' said the general. 'If you please, my dear fellow,' he added, turning to his adjutant, quite a graceful young man of pleasant appearance, 'order the bay filly to be led round here! Now you'll see for yourselves.' At this point the general drew on his pipe and blew out the smoke: 'Her condition isn't too good as yet: this damned hole of a town has no decent stables. But she's a, puff, puff, very respectable horse!'

'And is it long, your Excellency, puff, puff, that you've been so good as to own her?' said Chertokutsky.

'Puff, puff, puff, well… puff, not so very long. It's only just two years since I got her from the stud!'

'And were you so good as to get her already broken in, or were you so good as to break her in here?'

'Puff, puff, pu, pu, pu-u-u-ff, here,' said the general, before disappearing altogether in smoke.

Meanwhile a soldier leaped out of the stable, the clatter of hooves was heard, and at last a second one appeared in white overalls and with an enormous black moustache, leading by the bridle a trembling and jittery horse, which, when it suddenly threw up its head, almost threw the now squatting soldier up into the air, moustache and all. 'Whoa, now, whoa, Agrafena Ivanovna!' he said, leading her right up to the porch.

The filly's name was Agrafena Ivanovna: strong and wild like a southern belle, she crashed her hooves against the wooden porch and came to a halt.

Lowering his pipe, the general began looking at Agrafena Ivanovna with a contented expression. The colonel himself, stepping down from the porch, took Agrafena Ivanovna by the muzzle. The major himself gave Agrafena Ivanovna's leg a rub, the others clicked their tongues.

Chertokutsky stepped down from the porch and went

round behind her. The soldier, standing to attention and holding the bridle, looked the visitors right in the eyes as if he wanted to jump into them.

'Very, very nice!' said Chertokutsky, 'a super horse! And may I enquire, your Excellency, what her action's like?'

'She has a good stride, only... the Devil knows... that fool of a doctor's assistant gave her some pills, and for two days now she hasn't stopped sneezing.'

'She's very, very nice. And do you have the appropriate conveyance, your Excellency?'

'Conveyance?... But she's a saddle horse.'

'I know that; but I asked your Excellency so as to find out whether you have the appropriate conveyance for use with your other horses.'

'Well, I don't have too many conveyances. I must confess to you, I've long wanted to have one of the modern carriages. I wrote about it to my brother, who's in St Petersburg at the moment, but I don't know if he'll send me one or not.'

'It seems to me, your Excellency,' remarked the colonel, 'there's no better carriage than a Viennese one.'

'You think right, puff, puff, puff.'

'I have an exceptional carriage, your Excellency, of genuine Viennese workmanship.'

'Which one? The one you came in?'

'Oh, no. That one's just for travelling about, strictly for my own little trips, but this other one... it's amazing, it's light as a feather, and when you get into it, it's just as if, with your Excellency's permission, your nanny were rocking you in a cradle.'

'Comfortable, I suppose?'

'Very, very comfortable; cushions, springs, all as if in a picture-book.'

'That's good.'

'And how roomy it is! That is, I've not seen anything like it, your Excellency. When I was in the army, I could fit ten bottles of rum and twenty pounds of tobacco into the boxes, and besides that I also had with me about six tunics, linen and two pipes, your Excellency, as long as tapeworms, with your permission, and you could fit a whole bull into the pockets.'

'That's good.'

'I paid four thousand for it, your Excellency.'

'It ought to be good, to judge by the price; and you bought it yourself?'

'No, your Excellency: it came to me by chance. It was my friend that bought it, a rare fellow, my childhood companion, you'd get on with him perfectly; our attitude was this: what's yours or what's mine, it makes no difference. I won it from him at cards. Would you care to do me the honour, your Excellency, of visiting me tomorrow for lunch, and you can take a look at the carriage at the same time.'

'I don't know what to say to that. Alone, somehow, I… Perhaps if you'll allow me to bring the gentlemen officers.'

'And I humbly beg the gentlemen officers too. Gentlemen, I shall consider it a great honour to have the pleasure of seeing you in my house!'

The colonel, the major and the other officers thanked him with a courteous bow.

'I myself am of the opinion, your Excellency, that if you're buying something, then it should be something good, for if it's no good, there's no point in acquiring it. Now at my place, when you do me the honour of visiting tomorrow, I'll show you certain things that I have myself acquired in the farming line.'

The general looked and blew smoke out of his mouth.

Chertokutsky was extremely pleased that he had invited the gentlemen officers to visit him; in his head he was already ordering pâtés and sauces now, glancing very cheerfully at the gentlemen officers, who for their part had also somehow redoubled their good disposition towards him, something that was evident from their eyes and the little sort of half-bowing movements of their bodies. Chertokutsky was more free and easy somehow when he strutted forward, and his voice adopted a relaxed tone: the expression of a voice laden with pleasure.

'There, your Excellency, you'll make the acquaintance of the lady of the house.'

'I'll be delighted,' said the general, stroking his moustache.

After this, Chertokutsky wanted to set off for home straight away so as to prepare everything in good time for receiving the guests at lunch the next day; he was even already on the point of taking his hat in his hands, but somehow it strangely transpired that he remained for a little while longer. In the meantime card-tables had already been set up inside. Soon the entire company had divided up into groups of four to play whist, and was scattered in various corners of the general's rooms.

Candles were brought in. Chertokutsky could not decide for a long time whether he should sit down to a game of whist or not. But when the gentlemen officers began inviting him, it seemed to him quite at odds with the rules of social conduct to refuse. He took a seat. Unnoticed, there appeared before him a glass of punch, which, forgetting himself, he drank down that very same minute. After playing two rubbers, Chertokutsky again found a glass of punch by his hand, which, also forgetting himself, he drank down, saying before he did so, 'It's time I went home, gentlemen, it really is time.' But again he took a seat for a second game as well. Meanwhile the conversation in various corners of the room went in thoroughly individual directions.

Those playing whist were quite taciturn, but the non-players, sitting to the side on sofas, conducted their own conversations. In one corner a staff-captain, with a cushion tucked under his side and a pipe between his teeth, was recounting his amorous adventures quite fluently and smoothly, and had completely gripped the attention of the circle that had gathered around him. One extremely fat landowner with short arms rather like two sprouting potatoes listened with an unusually sweet expression, and only occasionally made an effort to put his short little arm behind his broad back to get out his snuffbox. In another corner quite a heated argument had started up about battle training, and Chertokutsky, who by this time had already twice put down a knave instead of a queen, suddenly began butting into other people's conversations and shouting from his corner 'in what year?' or 'of which regiment?', without noticing that at times his question had absolutely nothing to do with the topic. Finally, a few minutes before supper, the whist drew to a close, but it still carried on verbally. And it seemed as if everybody's head was full of whist. Chertokutsky remembered very well that he had won a lot, but he didn't pick anything up in his hands, and on rising from the table he stood for a long time in the position of a man who has no handkerchief in his pocket. In the meantime supper was served. It goes without saying that there was no shortage of wine and that Chertokutsky, because a bottle stood both to the right of him and to the left, was obliged at times almost involuntarily to pour some into his glass.

The conversation at table dragged on for a very long time,

yet it was conducted in a rather strange way. One landowner who had served in the 1812 campaign told of a battle that had never been, and then, for what reasons is completely unknown, he took the stopper from a carafe and stuck it into a cream cake. In a word, it was already three o'clock when they began to disperse, and the coachmen had to pick some individuals up in their arms as though they were bundles of shopping, and, while sitting in his carriage, Chertokutsky, for all his aristocratic ways, kept on bowing so low and with such swings of the head, that when he arrived home he brought two burrs with him in his moustache.

Absolutely everything was asleep in the house; the coachman was scarcely able to find the valet, who led his gentleman through the dining-room and handed him over to a housemaid, in whose wake Chertokutsky somehow reached the bedroom before getting into bed beside his pretty young wife, who was lying in the most delightful manner wearing a nightdress as white as snow. The movement induced by her husband falling onto the bed woke her. Stretching, lifting her lashes, and rapidly screwing up her eyes three times, she then opened them with a half-angry smile; but seeing that he definitely did not wish on this occasion to render her any affection, she turned in annoyance onto the other side and, laying her fresh cheek on her hand, she fell asleep soon after him.

It was already the sort of time that isn't called early in the countryside when the young mistress awoke beside her snoring husband. Remembering that he had returned home after three o'clock the night before, she didn't like to wake him, and after putting on the bedroom slippers that her husband had ordered for her from St Petersburg, and wearing a white chemise that draped itself around her like flowing water, she went through into her dressing-room, washed in water as fresh as herself, and went up to the dressing-table. She glanced at herself a couple of times and saw that she looked very pretty today. This seemingly insignificant circumstance forced her to sit in front of the mirror for precisely two extra hours. Finally she got dressed very sweetly and went out to freshen herself up in the garden. As if on purpose, the weather then was as beautiful as it can only be on a southern summer's day. The sun at noon burnt with all the strength of its rays, but it was cool strolling beneath the dark, dense lines of trees along the pathways, and the flowers, warmed by the sunshine, trebled their fragrance. The pretty little mistress completely forgot that it was already twelve o'clock and her husband was still sleeping. She could already hear the postprandial snoring of the two coachmen and the postilion, asleep in the stable that stood beyond the garden. But she continued to sit in the dense shade of a tree-lined pathway from which there was a clear view of the main road, gazing absent-mindedly at its unpopulated emptiness, when suddenly her attention was attracted by the dust that had appeared in the distance. Peering at it, she soon caught sight of several conveyances. In front drove a light two-seater; in it sat the general, with thick epaulettes glinting in the sun, and alongside him the colonel. There followed behind it a second carriage, a four-seater; in it sat the major and the general's adjutant with two more officers opposite them; behind this carriage followed the regimental droshky, familiar to all, on this occasion in the possession of the corpulent major; behind the droshky was a four-seater *bon-voyage*, in which there sat four officers with a fifth on their laps, and behind the *bon-voyage* were three officers cutting a dash on fine, darkly dappled bay horses.

'Surely they're not on their way to us?' thought the lady of the house. 'Oh, my God! They have indeed turned onto the bridge!' She shrieked, threw up her hands and ran across the flower-beds and the flowers straight into her husband's bedroom. He was dead to the world.

'Get up, get up! Get up, quickly!' she cried, tugging him by the arm.

'Eh?' said Chertokutsky, stretching, and without opening his eyes.

'Get up, honey-bunny! Do you hear? We've got guests!'

'Guests, what guests?' Saying this, he let out the little mooing noise that a calf makes when searching with its muzzle for its mother's teats. 'Mm...' he moaned, 'stretch out your neck, sweetie-pie, and I'll give you a kiss!'

'Darling, for God's sake get up, quickly! The general and the officers! Oh, my God, you've got burrs in your moustache!'

'The general? Ah, so he's already on his way? The Devil take it, why on earth did nobody wake me. And lunch, what about lunch, is everything properly ready?'

'What lunch?'

'Didn't I order it, then?'

'You? You got home at four o'clock in the morning, and however many questions I asked, you didn't say a thing to me. I didn't wake you up, honey-bunny, because I felt sorry for you: you'd had no sleep at all...' These last words she pronounced in an extremely languorous and beseeching voice.

Chertokutsky lay for a minute on the bed with his eyes open wide as if he had been struck by a thunderbolt. Finally he leaped up from the bed in nothing but his shirt, forgetting that this was not at all decent.

'Oh, I'm an ass!' he said, striking himself on the forehead. 'I invited them to lunch. What's to be done? How close are they?'

'I don't know… They should be arriving at any moment.'

'Darling!… Hide!… Hey, who's there? You, girl, come here, what are you afraid of, you idiot, the officers will be here at any moment. Tell them the master isn't at home, and say he won't be here at all, he drove off early this morning, do you hear? And let all the yard-servants know. Go on, quickly!'

Saying this, he hurriedly grabbed his dressing-gown and ran to hide in the coach-house, assuming his situation there to be quite safe. But when he got into the corner of the coach-house he saw that even here he might somehow be seen. 'That'll be better,' flashed through his mind, and in a moment he had thrown down the steps of the carriage standing nearby, leaped inside, closed the doors behind him, covered himself for greater security with the apron and the leather and fallen absolutely quiet, hunched up in his dressing-gown.

Meanwhile the conveyances had drawn up to the porch.

The general got out and gave himself a shake, followed by the colonel, adjusting the plume on his hat. Next the fat major leaped down from the droshky, clutching his sabre under his arm. Then the slim second lieutenants jumped out of the *bon-voyage* with the ensign who had been sitting on their laps, and finally the officers who had been cutting a dash on horseback stepped down from the saddles.

'The master's out,' said the footman, emerging onto the porch.

'What do you mean, out? He'll presumably be back by lunchtime, though?'

'No sir. He's gone off for the whole day. He'll only be back perhaps around this time tomorrow.'

'Well how about that!' said the general. 'How can it be?…'

'I must say, it's quite something,' said the colonel with a laugh.

'Well no, how could anybody do a thing like that?' continued the general in displeasure. 'Pah!… Damnation… If you can't entertain people, why invite them?'

'I don't understand, your Excellency, how anyone could do it,' said one young officer.

'What?' said the general, who was in the habit of always uttering this interrogative particle when speaking to anyone beneath the rank of major.

'I was saying, your Excellency, how could anyone behave in such a way.'

'Naturally… Well if he couldn't make it, or something – he might at least have let us know, or else not asked us.'

'Well then, your Excellency, there's nothing for it, let's go back again!' said the colonel.

'It stands to reason, there's no other way. But we can take a look at the carriage anyway, even without him. I don't suppose he's taken it with him. Hey, who's there, you, fellow, come here!'

'What can I do for you?'

'Are you the stableman?'

'I am, your Excellency.'

'Show us the new carriage your master got hold of recently.'

'Please come into the coach-house!'

The general went into the coach-house together with the officers.

'If you please, I'll wheel it out a little, it's a bit dark here.'

'That's enough, that's enough, good!'

The general and the officers walked all round the carriage and gave the wheels and springs a thorough inspection.

'Well, it's nothing special,' said the general. 'It's the most ordinary carriage.'

'The most unprepossessing,' said the colonel. 'Absolutely

nothing good about it.'

'I don't think it's worth four thousand at all, your Excellency,' said one of the young officers.

'What?'

'I'm saying I don't think it's worth four thousand, your Excellency.'

'What do you mean, four thousand! It's not even worth two! It's got nothing at all. Unless there's something special inside… If you please, my good man, undo the leather…'

And the eyes of the officers were presented with Chertokutsky, sitting hunched up in his dressing-gown in an extraordinary way.

'Ah, you're here!…' said the astonished general.

Whereupon the general immediately slammed the doors shut, covered Chertokutsky up again with the apron and departed along with the gentlemen officers.

NOTES

1. In Greek mythology, Philemon and Baucis were an extremely poor old couple who showed such great hospitality when visited by Zeus and Hermes in disguise that they were offered the chance to choose their reward; their choice was to be allowed to die at the same time.

BIOGRAPHICAL NOTE

Nikolai Gogol was born in 1809 in Sorochintsy (in Ukraine) to parents of Cossack descent. His father, a keen writer, penned a number of plays, sketches and poems, and it was whilst he was still at school that Gogol wrote his first works.

In 1829 Gogol moved to St Petersburg. Engaged first as a member of the civil service, and then as a history teacher and private tutor, he there became increasingly involved in the literary circles of his day. He made the acquaintance of Pushkin in 1831, and theirs was a friendship that was to last until Pushkin's death in 1837.

Although his early poetry had met with no success, in 1835 Gogol went on to pen two collections of writings – *Mirgorod* and *Arabesques* – both of which deal with decay, be it social or psychological. From 1836 until 1848 Gogol lived mainly abroad, and it was during this time that he worked on his masterpiece, the comic epic *Dead Souls*. The first part was published in 1842, but, following the advice of a priest who denounced his writing as sinful, and due to a deepening spiritual crisis, Gogol burnt the manuscript of the second part. Ten days later, in February 1852, he died.

Hugh Aplin studied Russian at the University of East Anglia and Voronezh State University. He worked at the Universities of Leeds and St Andrews before taking up his current post as Head of Russian at Westminster School, London.

HESPERUS PRESS – 100 PAGES

Hesperus Press, as suggested by the Latin motto, is committed to bringing near what is far – far both in space and time. Works written by the greatest authors, and unjustly neglected or simply little known in the English-speaking world, are made accessible through new translations and a completely fresh editorial approach. Through these short classic works, each little more than 100 pages in length, the reader will be introduced to the greatest writers from all times and all cultures.

For more information on Hesperus Press, please visit our website: **www.hesperuspress.com**

To place an order, please contact:
Grantham Book Services
Isaac Newton Way
Alma Park Industrial Estate
Grantham
Lincolnshire NG31 9SD
Tel: +44 (0) 1476 541080
Fax: +44 (0) 1476 541061
Email: orders@gbs.tbs-ltd.co.uk

SELECTED TITLES FROM HESPERUS PRESS

Gustave Flaubert *Memoirs of a Madman*
Alexander Pope *Scriblerus*
Ugo Foscolo *Last Letters of Jacopo Ortis*
Anton Chekhov *The Story of a Nobody*
Joseph von Eichendorff *Life of a Good-for-nothing*
Mark Twain *The Diary of Adam and Eve*
Giovanni Boccaccio *Life of Dante*
Victor Hugo *The Last Day of a Condemned Man*
Joseph Conrad *Heart of Darkness*
Edgar Allan Poe *Eureka*
Emile Zola *For a Night of Love*
Daniel Defoe *The King of Pirates*
Giacomo Leopardi *Thoughts*
Franz Kafka *Metamorphosis*
Herman Melville *The Enchanted Isles*
Leonardo da Vinci *Prophecies*
Charles Baudelaire *On Wine and Hashish*
William Makepeace Thackeray *Rebecca and Rowena*
Wilkie Collins *Who Killed Zebedee?*
Théophile Gautier *The Jinx*
Charles Dickens *The Haunted House*
Luigi Pirandello *Loveless Love*
Fyodor Dostoevsky *Poor People*
E.T.A. Hoffmann *Mademoiselle de Scudéri*
Henry James *In the Cage*
Francesco Petrarch *My Secret Book*
D.H. Lawrence *The Fox*
Percy Bysshe Shelley *Zastrozzi*